Ranger

Trista Vaporblade

Copyright © 2014 Trista Vaporblade
Cover Illustration Copyright © 2014 Robert Wilson
All rights reserved.
ISBN-13: 978-1499295696
ISBN-10: 1499295693

For the four pre-readers of my prologue, who dared to take a chance before the proofies got a hold of it and made sure it was safe – Robert Wilson: who can do the most amazing things with a computer! Joshua Jansen: who took the time to check out my Facebook page and shared some of his writing with me. Caleb Baker: who had ideas for this book to be called "The Lone Rangerette." X) And last but not least, JM Christian: an amazing writer and faithful reader. I raise my hat in thanks to each of you.

"Friendship is born at that moment when one person says to another: "What! You too? I thought I was the only one."
-C. S. Lewis

CONTENTS

~

Prologue - 5

Chapter 1 - 11

Chapter 2 - 24

Chapter 3 - 35

Chapter 4 - 41

Chapter 5 - 49

Chapter 6 - 56

Chapter 7 - 67

Chapter 8 - 80

Chapter 9 - 102

Chapter 10 - 117

Chapter 11 - 130

Chapter 12 - 141

Chapter 13 - 153

Chapter 14 - 165

Chapter 15 - 177

Chapter 16 - 186

Chapter 17 - 197

Chapter 18 - 204

Chapter 19 - 215

Chapter 20 - 224

Chapter 21 - 230

Epilogue - 237

Prologue

"Do ya know what this is?" I glance over, careful to keep the light off the left side of my face, allowing my hat's brim to overshadow most of my features.

I roll the object in question around between my thumb and forefinger, letting the light from the bartender's lanterns glisten off the shiny outer layer. I nod only slightly — the man probably won't catch it — and place the small, oblong shape back onto the smooth counter top. I send it twirling slowly back toward him with a flick of my hand. "It's a silver bullet, isn't it?" Although I've never seen one, the metal shell makes it clear; of course I know what it is.

The filthy rancher grunts, probably upset I know the answer to something he's been stumped about for days.

The man is repulsive: dirt smears, tobacco stains, torn and fraying shirt. I try not to noticeably scoot too far back on my bar stool. Why had he approached me anyway? I'd come here, into town, to visit the saloon, to dig up gossip, and to learn what I could from the natives of a certain family who had once lived here. I need information.

The man stuffs the glimmering bullet back into his shirt pocket and re-seats himself on the stool directly beside me. I shift to the left. He raises a large, stained hand and mumbles at the man behind the thick counter. I watch in silence as he receives his libation; probably not the first he's had today. I shake my head when offered a drink; my mind needs to be clear. I have business to attend to.

I shift on my seat so I can lean my elbows on the bar; my hat is pulled down low so only my eyes shine out from underneath the dark fabric. I do a sweep through the mass of what I can only assume are the regulars, watching, assessing them all. I need to find the right someone, that certain person who'll open up to a stranger without hesitation.

I must know about that night.

The man beside me transfers his ample bulk off the stool and to his feet. He turns his cold, beady eyes back to me. I clench my jaw. I've stood unflinching before mountain lions and coyotes, I've held my ground when they charge, but somehow this man has accomplished what they could not; my nerves are on edge. People and I don't get along.

"Where ya come from, stranger?" The rancher finally disrupts the uncomfortable silence. He knows. I can hear it in his voice. He knows I'm not what I seem to be. "Where ya headed? Lookin' fer work, I'll reckon." He tosses his head back, along with the mug he holds, downing the contents.

He slings the glass to the counter top and smears the back of one hand across his mouth. "And how comes ya wear such clothes? What are ya hidin'?" His tone is now probing and accusing. From the corner of my eye, I find him bearing down on me; closer, ever closer.

My head snaps around, and even though he can't see my entire face, I let my eyes do the talking. He backs off, albeit only slightly. "I need answers," I hiss out. I've run out of time and patience. "And I need them now."

His face goes slack and he shrugs. "There are plenty o' us who can tell ya things. Things no one else would dare say they know. Though I don't reckon we'd tell an outsider."

I pull myself from the seat; sitting I had been taller than him, but now I loomed. I suppose I look a bit intimidating, for he shrinks back a little farther. "Every man has his price," I say quietly.

I can see his Adam's apple bob, even under all the excess skin. He nods slowly. "What's ya want to know?" He matches my tone, secretive and cautious.

"I want to know about September fifth, 1849. I want to know about the Rangers." I state it flatly, without emotion, while inside my heart pumps like a bellows. But I feel nothing.

The man draws away even more, his eyes wide. I stand completely frozen; he thinks I'm joking, or else mad. But I know I'm not.

Gradually he moves back to his original position and leans over the bar, motioning me close with a quick signal of his head. I come, hesitantly at first but then I know this may be my only chance. I won't let it slip through my hands.

"Ya wanna know 'bout the killing?" He nods faintly at his own question. "Ya wan'a know 'bout them?" I don't bother to respond; he knows I do.

A hush falls over us once more; I observe the men in the background playing cards, laughing, joking. I vaguely wonder to myself exactly how they can be so lighthearted when something so terrible had occurred and could happen again.

"I don't know much, barely anythin' compared to some who've already gone ta their graves." He runs a nervous finger around the rim of his mug, peering into it with uneasy eyes. "But I'll tell ya this, fella' – don't get assorted up in it. They say whoever does goes a missin'; some found dead, killed in 'orrible ways."

I exhale audibly, irritated. A warning is not what I had come looking for. "Tell me all you know." He scowls as if I've cuffed him. "I can pay..." He twists his head the other direction. "In gold." His shoulders blades roll, and he stands up straighter.

"Sorry, missy." He grins up at me and I can make out several missing teeth. "I's been told not to harken to foreigners. And what good's a reward, if'n yer passed on before ya use it." He claps the mug down on the counter, flings a small, rusty coin behind it, and saunters toward the door.

I stare at the table top. He knew.

I pivot on one heel and bound after him. As he reaches the double hinged entrance, I clench him firmly by the shoulders and swing him up against the wall. "Tell me what you know," I seethe out between my teeth. Most of the heads in the room that had been pointing our way now turn back to their games – just a friendly exchange between two of the ranchers. Or not so friendly.

The man passes his hands over his face to shield it, advance protection from any blows I might attempt to use. "I'm tellin' ya, there's naught to know." He's groveling now.

I raise my clenched fist from his right shoulder. I won't hit him, but I need to hear what he's holding back.

"No, no!" He waves his arms in a fit of hysterics, as if they would save him had my intentions been to truly hurt him. "Look, the Rangers, they weres the governor and 'is family, ya see. They took off one day on a stage coach headed north; no one knows why. The only thin' everybody understands is the coach never made it ta the big city; not even the driver nor the horses. It just all up'n vanished and heaven only knows if'n any of 'em really survived the murder." I drop my hands, leaving a crumpled wad of fabric where my tight fists had clenched his shirt.

"Though I've heard tales that say a child escaped the killin', the lone Ranger ta get away with 'is life." I back away, my eyes locked on his churning jaw. "I also he'rd it told that he died, not long after, from a wound he received. But one day he'll be back, ta kill off them beasts that took 'is family." My eyes snap angrily at him and he begins to panic again. "But that's all I know." He gulps and swiftly slips to the door. Then he's gone and I hear the faint pounding of horse's hooves over the sandy dust.

So they were all dead then, each and every one. All the Rangers, the entire family. I release a pent-up breath and exit the saloon, leaving the trace of mixed feelings in my wake. This was it, the answer to so many questions. Somehow I'd always known, but now there was no running from it.

I loose the reins from the hitching post and swing to my mount's empty back. He nickers, and we set off toward the north, toward my home.

My thoughts swim in untold waves that thrash upon the shores of my mind.

So they say I've died. They think I'm lost to this world. They call me the lone Ranger. They even say I'll come back and save them from the lethal creatures that roam these parts.

They say this is who I am.

Nothing could be farther from the truth.

Chapter 1
Several Years Earlier

The stage coach's rear wheel bounced over a deep rut that cut down into the road's soft path, sending jolting tremors though each of the passengers confined within. Kimberly's head lurched downward into her mother's thin shoulder, and she woke with a sudden start. A soft, apologetic look was directed her way, as if it might be the source from where healing would come to ease the new, throbbing sting in her ear. But more than her physical discomfort she felt keenly the hollow ache in her heart, and what could anything do for that?

Kim blinked weary eyes into the murky glow that shone at patchy intervals over the trees and in through the only window of their carriage; even the moon appeared somber on this night. She trembled and tugged at the corners of the knitted shawl, drawing it up tighter about her narrow shoulders. How she hated her life.

Kim pressed as far back into her seat as possible. Closing her eyes, she struggled to still her own shivering. In the semi-hush she could make out the echo of the horses' rapid hoof beats drumming against the turf, the wagon wheels grinding about their axles, and the coachman clicking to his animals to hasten their gait. She imagined her father sharing a look with her mother and nodding. She could hear the hum of her younger sister's rhythmic snores and their little brother's tiny whimpers just above the bouncing clatter of the coach. Oh, how she desired to spring from the carriage at that moment and have all her anxieties washed away. If only dreams came true.

Five hours before, her life had been that of the governor's daughter in a dusty western settlement; now she was the promised bride-to-be, betrothed to a haughty snob who belonged to a society where ladies only existed to launder their hair and groom their domesticated kitties. What kind of a life was that? Kim sighed inwardly.

Though she was small in almost every way and delicate in appearance, Kimberly Ranger was not a being meant for the enclosed life, and most certainly not with other senseless girls who flitted about like tame parakeets. *'No,'* Kim exhaled. *'I was created for the outdoors; for the creeks and the rivers, the birds and the sky. I was formed for more than this life of seclusion and captivity. This is only what my father desires, what he is handing me over to.'*

Now she wished her world had been shaped differently, that she'd been born the offspring of a rancher, a blacksmith, or even a mercantile owner. But no, she had the blessing of being born to the governor, the eldest of his children, which meant when the official from the city had called upon her father to request her hand for his son, the governor had little hesitation on the matter. But there was something more than just her legitimacy to be married, something concerning the town they'd just abandoned.

Her father had always hidden things from her about the place they'd lived, things linked to the area and its past. She'd overheard him conversing with their mother, speaking about a presence that haunted the prairies and roamed through the timbers. Whatever it was, he'd talked as if it were deadly. Kim supposed, perhaps that was one of the explanations for his eagerness to give her away; he was entrusted with a secret and he wanted out, badly.

A frosty gust ruffled the window's scant covering. The wafting breeze soared into their box-like compartment and whipped auburn hair around her face. With one hand, Kim peeled back the taut curtain and leaned forward to gaze out at the passing darkness.

They had just entered into the forest; the stoic, silent trees breaking up out of the road to climb their stiff way toward the shady heavens. To Kim they appeared as rough, bloodless fingers grasping hungrily for something they could not obtain. She shuddered.

Shadows darted through the endlessly increasing population of the timberland, wrapping their sticky bodies to coarse tree limbs only to fall away as the stage coach passed by. *'If only I were a shadow.'* Kim found herself fantasizing with longing. *'To pass where one would without thought and glide free without chains to hold you down. No bonds to keep you back.'*

She was about to let the paper-thin drapery go, when she caught sight of something peculiar. At first it was only a glint in the murk, a lighter gray against the black. Then the horses began to snort. They strained at their tethers, and the coach was sent lurching forward, hard.

As the mares bolted into a gallop, Kim was abruptly tossed a few inches out the window, her knees crashing hard into the side of the door. Lightheaded, she blinked at the swirling scenery that was spiraling past and saw dull outlines, animals of some kind, racing along beside them through the woods, darting in and out of view. Wild cats? Or were they dogs with the maddening disease? She felt hands snatching at her, towing her back into the cabin and into her mother's arms. Fine, gentle fingers stroked her hair, quiet voices spoke her name, but her mind was captive elsewhere. What lay beyond the barrier of these four walls? What was prowling out there in the gloom?

An eerie chill stole over her and slowly crept up her spine, the hairs on the back of her neck rose. Somewhere out there a creature screamed, long and resonating in the bitter cool of the night. The horses reached out for all that was left in them, the coach throttling on along the crude path.

Kim pulled away from her mother, her legs wobbling with the carriage's uneven posture. She was certain the wheels were fixing to remove themselves, or that the horses in their distraught state would slam them into a tree. What was it that was chasing them? Or was it even pursuing them?

Suddenly the left-hand side of the coach shuddered to a dead halt while the right half rocketed forward at an angle. Kimberly's feet lost contact with the base boards and she went sprawling headlong to the floor, the breath knocked from her lungs. She cried out in distress, but there was no wind in her throat to carry the sound past her lips. She choked back a second mute scream and tried to suppress the terror that was propelling her heart into a faster beat.

Something heavy thudded to the ground as they spun about in the wild twist, and Kim was sure they'd lost the driver. The stagecoach finished its mad jaunt with jarring impact, crashing sidelong into something massively solid. The two narrow doors on either end popped open, bouncing once or twice on their hinges before lying still – like the rest of the world about them. Everything was motionless. The ordinary evening resonance had dropped into a hush; even the horses ceased their nervous movement. No more screams, no more breathing; just vacant silence.

Kim watched her father from her prone posture on the floor; he gradually drew closer to the exit hatch, peering out searchingly. She followed him with her eyes as he begin to rise from the bench, then recoiled in alarm as something powerful gripped the upper portion of his body, ripping the man from the carriage and tilting the coach at a precarious angle. The creature was black as midnight, larger than a full-grown man, and had wide eyes the color of fresh blood.

Her mother's tingling cry brought Kim's head snapping around. Her heart soared into what she was sure must have been failure speed as both her mother and little brother shot backward out of the carriage. With finality, she noted that her younger sister had also vanished; she was alone in the death box.

Once again silence reigned supreme and Kim lay frozen in shock. Nothing more than a sloped-sideways stage coach with gaping doorways on opposite ends met her faltering gaze. She shivered, gradually bracing herself on weak elbows, hoping to eventually make it to her feet.

Something rapidly flickered past the open hatch, the one that angled closer to the ground, sending a stiff breeze whispering through the carriage. Kim instinctively wrinkled her nose at the stagnant odor that piggybacked the wind. Pushing hastily to her knees, Kim skulked toward the other exit. She had to get out. If she didn't, the creature would climb in after her and forcefully remove her.

An enormous face stared in through the yawning opening below, and although she couldn't discern any features but the fluid, crimson eyes in the shadowy night, Kim was convinced her panic would smother her into oblivion. The being shifted and so did Kim. Her feet were finally beneath her and they began to move of their own accord. Bounding forward, she hooked a leg over the frame to the door that pointed skyward. Overhead the icy, callous moon laughed down upon her.

She tossed the next leg over and dropped with a dull thud to the furrowed trail. Her knees buckled inward and she crumpled to the dirt streaked earth, but her agile hands were under her, pushing her back up. Kim ran, her mind still having trouble catching up with her body's actions. She didn't know where she was headed, but her shoes dug deep into the topsoil and her legs drove her onward. A last look over her shoulder at the coach confirmed her worries, the thing was worming its way through the top hatch; it was coming after her.

Kim's hands rose up in front of her body and face to ward off the slapping branches and the warm, sticky spider webs; her calf-high boots crunched down on endless dozens of dead leaves, tore through numerous bramble patches, and leapt with trembling confidence over bent and warped wooden logs. Her awareness was indistinct; the boundaries of her mind finding they no longer had limits to which they must adhere to. Two things alone penetrated through, piercing the haze: her parents, and likely her younger siblings, were gone. The beasts who'd murdered them were now pursuing her, and they would stalk her until they'd slain their prey. She discerned the latter point with absolute certainty.

Kim couldn't tell how far she'd run, nor did she have an inkling as to where she was, but she knew it was behind her; she could hear it. The immense paws drumming through the crisp undergrowth, the exaggerated panting of the enormous creature. It blocked all other noise out like a blanket of enclosed echoes.

Her leg muscles burned, the soles of her feet ached, and her lungs felt as if they would explode from exertion. She gasped in long, ragged breaths; perspiration weaved down her brow and into her stricken eyes despite the frosty air that encircled her. For a fleeting instant she bothered to speculate: would anyone ever know about this night? Would someone discover her body after the creature had done its work? Would anybody even care? She suspected her husband-to-be would not so much as shed a tear; he would merely find another, more convenient girl to wed.

Kimberly sensed the beast pull away; she felt the monstrous presence depart from the forest walks behind her. Spinning her head to look, she continued her wild flight. Where had it gone? Her right boot caught under a rotten log and she went stumbling headlong into the dead foliage that littered the ground. A flurry of tan, brittle leaves bloomed up around her like a russet water cloud. Kim's head snapped forward, almost connecting with the carpeted earth, her arms buried up to her elbows in the brown, broken fronds. Leisurely, like rain from heaven, the leaves drifted back down to nestle upon her sloppily braided head. Smaller strands of hair had dragged themselves away from the tri-stranded weave and now hung about her face as an auburn curtain. She blew the renegade locks aside, lying for a moment on her stomach in the lustrous light of the pale moon. Inhaling taut gulps of the frigid air, she watched as the they returned to the forest night in clouds of puffy white.

Beyond the trees just ahead, a clearing of empty grass arose. A ring of short, narrow saplings bordered the circumference of the circle and gradually gave way to the loftier, more prominent ones. Kim struggled to her feet and scurried into the banded glade, something about it almost making her feel safe. With this sensation dominating her mind, she wandered toward the center of the clearing and hunkered down in the swaying weeds. Drawing her knees up to her chest, she gazed at the star-scattered sky high above. Her breathing slackened as she fought far less to bring the air in. Her slight form began to quiver and shake with the unkind evening chill; the trees rustled their lanky limbs all around her as the gusts of wind whiffled through their boughs.

Finally, her mind began to clear; the mad chase through the woods had thrown most everything except the thought to survive aside. Now, in this calm place, the moments in the coach came back with forceful clarity. In a matter of seconds she had gone from the pledged governor's daughter to the trembling orphan who would cease to exist after this night. Her body began to sway; it quavered with more than just the cold now. Tears coursed their salty tracks across her flushed cheeks and sobs beset her slender frame. There was no one to whom she could go if somehow she escaped this. No relations of any sort to offer her aid. Her father had told her their family was the last of the Rangers, which now meant she was all there was left of the bloodline. The only Ranger left in this solitary realm. And she would not be here for much longer.

Suddenly she regretted the longings she'd expressed from the safety of the coach; her feelings had all too well become reality. She had desired her life to be changed; she'd wanted to leap from the carriage and run from it all. Well, she had. *'It was my fault.'* Kim found she was blaming the deaths of them all upon herself; it was her own doing. She had seen the beasts before they attacked, pursuing the coach; she should have said something.

Not certain as to how long she had been sitting there, Kim scrubbed at her running nose and weepy eyes with a hand, beginning to gaze around. Where was she? Why hadn't the creature come and taken her? From the corner of one eye she caught sight of something bone-white that shone in the moon's amber radiance. Kim spun swiftly, stumbling backward as she rose; afraid the beast had come at last. But all that met her stare was a lonely, wooden cross whose pallid paint had begun to flake off and lumber edges start to splinter. Tentatively she stepped nearer, tracing a hand over the coarse surface. It offered her conviction; she was undeniably still here and that which had transpired was reality, not some troubled dream she had conjured.

The ancient cross undoubtedly was a marker for a grave. Any other time Kim would have been noticeably disturbed to be standing by or on a burial site; tonight, however, it gave a kind of peace. A token allowing her to realize she was yet among the living and there might still be hope.

Kim inhaled deeply and swallowed. Somehow she had to manage a way out of this glade and back to the settlement. Certainly someone there would assist her. Perhaps one of the older folks who her father had employed could show her a place where she could work for food. But then, she was getting ahead of herself. She first needed to get away without being ambushed.

Kim turned a tight circle, observing the possibilities of an escape route. Which direction was back? Then she caught sight of them, the identical, unblinking eyes watching her. Their bloodshot glow soaked into her petrified mind, burning into her memory. Kimberly heaved in a ragged breath; the animal wasn't coming in after her. For some unusual reason it feared the light, or the clearing itself.

A threatening snarl swelled up from behind and Kim jerked about to discover another pair of luminescent eyes fixed upon her. Gradually, more joined the first two at the tree line. She pivoted from side to side; all around her dwindling sanctuary, the creatures were gathered, each of them waiting. She cowered and stooped down by the cross, her trembling hands clinging to the point where the beams intersected. There would be no going back, no place to run. She was trapped, encircled on every side; she was as good as dead.

A paw that resembled a dense section of firewood rather than an appendage struck at her; lengthy claws extended, and shredded through her dress's sleeve. Kim shrieked and scrambled to the center of the ring. She had been mistaken; the beasts would eventually gain the courage they required to fight through whatever it was keeping them at bay. They would come for her.

Another creature swept its extended arm at Kim. Catching her hair in its talons, it yanked back, pulling her face-first into the grass and leaves, her cry muffled in the earth. From all edges they began to attack, to lash out. Bit by bit they moved ever nearer, but not once did anything more than paws and claws issue forth from the tree line.

Kim sat huddled in the clearing, knees to her chest. She cried out in fear every time the air was displaced by a hairy arm. The claws winged over and around her, some catching on her dress and tearing through. Again and again the beasts plagued her with batterings, until finally one cuffed her solidly across the cheek with outspread claws.

Warm, crimson liquid began to dribble and then stream down her agonized face and along her neck. Kim screamed as the pain overtook the blood and her hands compressed her torn flesh. An elongated, even slice split her cheek from the lobe of her left ear all the way to her jaw in a diagonal stripe. The searing fluid oozed out between her splayed fingers and dripped to the ground, staining her clothing and the weeds around her knees in a thin stream of red.

She dumbly tore at the hem of her dress, ripping a section off with her nails. Gathering the cloth in one palm, she plastered it to her cheek; her face felt as if the entire left side was being hacked off. Kimberly cried out again, but found the working of her mouth made the cut flex open, triggering additional torture. She bit her lip before the next yell of anguish toiled its way past her throat.

The creatures seemed to be energized by the sight of the crimson liquid, lifting their voices in howls, screams, and cries of bloodlust. They desired to kill her. No longer was it a command; it was a need. Snapping their massive jaws in the air, they ripped away at nothing in a vain effort to break through the invisible bonds that held them back.

Kim's head grew fuzzy and started to swim, her eyes flickering in and out from silver to black. Gradually the beast's yelps seeped away into silence and the world around her became a miner's shaft with the light put out. Infinite darkness pressed down on her and blood pooled around her skull in a boundless flood.

Chapter 2

Kimberly's eyelids fluttered open, and she sat up quickly. Intense pain shot down the left side of her face, a hand flying instinctively to her cheek. Ragged cloth bound around her face and jaw bone, as well as wrapping around her ear. Kim's mind cleared the smoky fog away, and she recalled the moments of extreme terror and the horrible misfortune that had befallen her family. Had it all been simply a coincidence? Whatever it was that had occurred, it was over and no amount of forged suppositions or false hopes could bring her parents and siblings back.

A plethora of voices rose in pitch outside the petite, cone-shaped shelter she'd woken in. Her eyes grew large with the realization that she was not back in town. Nor was this the glade she'd stumbled into the night of the catastrophe. Someone must have discovered her body, brought her here, bound her wound, and let her live. At least for the moment.

Kim pushed the tanned deer hide aside and scooted forward on her knees toward the shelter's outer tent flap. The space inside the lodge was cramped, so it only took a moment before the treated skin of a large animal was in her hands. Kim pressed the flap away from the rest of the tent just enough to see out with a single eye.

The strong scent of tanning leather and skins invaded the air around her; Kim breathed deeply of the old, rough scent. Before her observing eye the world of another people blossomed: awnings and shelters like her own squatted in the dirt all around in a sort of semi-circle, each hut seeming to lure the attention toward the inner ring of lodges where a grassy patch of earth was occupied by an animal-hide canopy stretched over a wooden frame. A fire pit lay mostly dormant before the tent, smoke squirming up toward the cloudless sky from the mound of stones, the flames having only recently been put out.

Near the outlying tepees that were raised closest to the woodlands women stirred, with long curved rods, the contents of black pots that dangled over their lesser fires. Children weaved in-between their parents. Sticks in hand, they dashed after one another, fighting off each other's fake attacks with their own stiff implements. The men and older boys sat cross-legged in small groups, sharpening spear points and shaping arrowheads. Some hauled in firewood for the women's cooking pits, laying it before the various rings of stone. Each individual wore animal hides draped over their darkly tanned bodies; breaches and vests for the men and long dresses for the women. They spoke in a strange, low murmur – it sounded of the steady rain pattering softly on a roof, of a stream's gentle lapping upon its shores, and yet it resonated in her a sort of alarm, for she could not understand what they said.

Recognition dawned upon her: these people were the native Indians. Their tribes had survived here for ages before the white people had even discovered this land's existence. Kim had only ever seen one of the dark-skinned folk before, and that at a far distance. Her father had ill-disposed feelings towards them and had brought the dealings with the clans to a standstill. He presumed them a troublesome lot and, Kim believed, if he had gotten his way would have run them right off the earth. She had never overheard him giving reason to his distastes; he simply didn't care for them. However, if they were the ones who had saved her, she had good reason to be grateful to them. At least for the moment.

Her limbs felt heavy and stiff as she rose, her shoulders stretching taut while her feet appeared somewhat bigger than normal; undoubtedly they were swollen from the night of the accident because of all the running. Kim shifted back and forth on her unsteady toes, she felt entirely off balance as if someone had taken her old body and given her a new one she wasn't accustomed to.

Flexing her hand open and closed, she wondered how these people had stolen her away from the creatures in the forest. What type of animals had they even been?

Kim rolled her shoulder blades and without further thought as to what she was doing – whether or not the Indians were friendly or what they intended to do with her – she parted the deer-skin flap and stepped out into the sunlit afternoon. The women glanced up from their steaming cauldrons, the young ones stilled their games of war, and the men let their hands drop to their sides and go slack. For a brief instant all was silent; everyone held their collective breath. Then the entire village came to life again as if struck by an invisible hand, each returning to their respective duties as if nothing had transpired, completely ignoring her.

Kim blinked several times in surprise, having anticipated something different than the reaction she had received. At least they weren't going to murder her where she stood; that was good. She took a cautious step forward. Her eyes caught a flurry of movement and her head spun toward it. A boy, who seemed only a little older than herself, came scampering into the group of tents, his dark face beaming. He jogged over to an elderly man who sat cross-legged on a brilliantly dyed blanket and began to bombard him with a string of lengthy sentences in their own tongue.

The youth quickly started to gesture with his hands, his animation becoming rather comical to her eyes. The man's wrinkled brow furrowed even more and he shrugged several times, appearing at a loss. The lad turned as if to continue his narrative with full physical actions, but as he caught sight of Kim the words died on his lips. She swallowed.

The boy shrugged off the old man's question as he began to stride toward her. For every pace he took she sensed her uncertainties swelling, until he stood before her, eye to eye. For some peculiar reason, as the lad lingered there, looking at her with a kind of wonder, she felt the anxiety depart and Kim straightened under his gaze. He quirked a sideways smile and nodded. "Yella isn'non u tesrant Asgaya-wahya." Kim elevated one eyebrow and he chuckled.

"You are strong to fight the poison of the Asgaya-wahya." He spoke in nearly unfaltering English. His forehead creased and he folded his well-muscled arms over his chest. "I regret that we did not find you sooner." He stopped himself from going on and motioned for her to reenter the tent she'd woken in.

Seeing refusal as pointless, Kim turned and withdrew back inside, deciding to follow his suggestion. This was his village after all; he knew what was expected of foreigners here. Kim tugged at her torn dress, the shredded hem swirling around her bare feet.

"My aunt has a spare pelt she will lend you once she has returned from hunting. Then we can burn this old garment." The boy explained, essentially reading her mind. He swept a basket from the side of the canvas lodge into his hand and positioned it next to the entry flap. "I am called Tonto, and this is the tribe of Hungdi, who is chief here."

"My name is Kim." She replied with more strength than she thought her voice could muster with the gash through her cheek. Somehow her

Ranger

words seemed to carry a deeper resonance then she remembered; her hand went to the bandage.

"Ah," Tonto said raising a finger, his eyes bright. "My old friend, Rashadi, did that for you. None other would have been able to save your life." He bent at the waist, stirring the ashes together with some twigs from the centrally positioned fire ring in the tipi. Smoke began to sift up the funnel-shaped covering, filtering toward a hole at the very top where it could withdraw into the outer world. He glanced over at Kim through the curtain of fog, his deep cobalt eyes appearing glossy in the weak light. His dark skin seemed almost black and his hair was a raven's wing that had settled upon his skull. "Sit and I will tell you how you came to be among us."

Kimberly seated herself directly across from the peculiar boy, in a cross-legged position; he seemed to share something with her. The way his eyes glazed, the manner in which his lips curved in a smile, he had something in common with her.

Tonto stirred the ember bed with a scrawny stick and traced the sparks with his gaze. "Night had fallen, impenetrable night, when the moon shines its face down from directly above and when the predators come from their dens to hunt. Sometimes I go out, far into the woods and I find a place where I can sit and think. I like to wait and watch in the darkness; to see and perceive things no other has yet understood or heard.

"I come most often to one spot in particular, and in an unseen position I listen and wait. Soon I overhear echoes as if from far away: breathing as in chase, panting as in haste, and I feel a presence that is wholly evil. I sense malice riding in the very air itself." Tonto snapped the twig in two with a single hand, his stare never flickering from the coals. "So I hid myself in the tallest of the trees, wondering what creature lay yonder and hoping beyond hope not to be seen. I knew I should flee; I ought to have run from that foul beast. But something inside kept me there and I continued to watch. Soon you came, stumbling into the exact place I had been settled not long before. You looked more than frightened; you appear petrified and ashen white. I watched as you wept, sobbing as if your heart was being torn out," He peered across the space between them. "I knew then that you'd lost something, but I thought if I came down you would flee; some creature had been pursuing you, a terrible fiend. Perhaps the very being who'd taken what you cherished, or maybe even the manifestation of everything you are most afraid of. So I delayed and I observed. You went to the cross and you clung to it, and still I remained where I was.

"The creatures came then, the Asgaya-wahya; I have only heard of them in legends, and though now I have seen them all that is seared to my memory are their eyes: blood seems to drip from them. These animals must destroy and their claws alone have slain more than all the spears and bows in this camp. I feared as I saw them, for you and for me. Then I beheld a mist of crimson, and you fell to rise no more. The beasts are ravenous. Whatever they are, they are driven by more than the need to kill; they live off of their cravings.

"I leapt down from my perch in the safety of the trees limbs, crying out an ancient saying my mother had taught me. My hands found a hefty branch and I swung it, snapping the wooden shaft over one of their ugly heads. My weapon gone they could have easily taken me, and you as well, but they fled." Tonto shook his head, obviously still bewildered by this turn of events.

"I slowly approached you and saw the cloth-doused wound on your face; the poisonous effect of the beast already taking hold on your small form. In my alarm I picked you up and carried you to Rashadi, a man with a mysterious understanding of medicines. He inspected the claw slash and said he didn't think he could save you — too much of the venom had already entered your body. But I pleaded with him, so he tried." Tonto outlined a path through the stoked embers with his broken twig, the sparks bouncing away from it. He let it slip from his grip into the powdery ashes and stared up at her. "He succeeded in sparing your life, though he could never restore you to the person you once were."

Kimberly sat in silence as the last words faded away, curling upward with the hazy air. She distrusted this boy. Why would he bother to weave such a tale? Was it to cause her confusion so that in this fragile state they could impose their savage ways on her? Something stirred deep within, and Kim knew his story was not meant for illusion. Her hand waveringly rose to her bandage again. She cringed. *'How have I changed?'* Her heart picked up speed. Eyes darting she saw sorrow pictured on the lad's face. "What has happened to me? What have you done?" Kim lurched backward and stood as swiftly as possible. "What has changed?" Her feet felt unusual, clumsy and awkward.

Tonto looked on with grief lacing his features. "Nothing that can be altered now." He spoke steadily, trying to ease her panic. "The people of this village, my kin, see you only as you are, not as you have been. They will accept you for what you are, which I cannot say for the people who used to know you."

Kimberly stepped away from the fire stones, her heels knocking into an iron kettle. "And what am I? What is wrong with me?" she breathed, scarcely above a whisper.

Tonto rose from his place near the coals, a solitary hand stretched out in a gesture for her to follow. "Come, I will show you." Kim swallowed painfully and made her way through the rawhide flap and out into the daylight behind him.

Tonto took the meandering route around the leather lodges, veering off to the right and out between the border tents that lay near the woods. Kim hesitated for only a moment before pacing from the safety of the camp; she needed to know what had happened.

Tonto led them under the thick, shadowy bows of the trees, continuing their trek in silence until the woods thinned and the saplings began to fan out around a brook of flowing water. The Indian lad pulled up beside the creek bed, gesturing Kim close. "Look." He directed, waving a hand over the surface of the stream.

Kim grimaced, her cheek flamed with discomfort. She grit her teeth together. Striding forward she stared down into the swirling, crystal liquid as it spun and rolled down the rocky shore in a slow babble. At first, she noticed nothing different about her features, aside from the ragged binding casing her face nothing appeared changed. Then, as Kim raised her fingers to push a stringy lock of hair away, she nearly gasped. So she had been affected by the creature's venom. If one had not known her before the accident one would not see anything abnormal. But Kim knew – she was bigger. Roughly two and a half heads taller, her wrists were thicker, her arms more heavily muscled, and her legs were stiff in their longer length. Kim found herself wobbling at the water's edge, her will to stand gave out and she sat firmly on the side of the riverbank. "How?" She whispered, running her palms over her biceps and gaping at her new build.

"The Asgaya-wahya's bite is lethal. Rashadi says, according to the myths, no one has ever survived it before. And what it would do to a small girl we did not know. You are very fortunate to even be breathing." Tonto said remaining in the forest shadows.

Her mind agreed with the boy, but her emotions rebelled. What had become of her existence? She would give anything to go back to that carriage ride and the awful prospect of an arranged marriage. So what if she was only a backstage implement of a man's fancies? At least she'd have a life. Now what did she have?

Ranger

Chapter 3

I can't remember how he got me out of that place by the river, with my tears flowing. I don't recollect what means he used to convince me to stay or by what method he persuaded me to speak again. All I can recall with perfect clarity from those days is the numbness, the cold, hollow sensation of an empty void that built up in my chest and threatened to overwhelm my entire being. Days passed, months and finally years.

I remember him, Tonto, coaxing me out from the silent shell that kept me cut off from the rest of the world. I can still picture the times when I would become extremely distraught and the cold would throb inside until it exploded into a boiling rage I didn't know I had. I have no memory of him teaching me to ride, and I don't know when he showed me how to use a sturdy bow and shoot the nocked shafts.

Sometimes my mind can't even recall the moment when he introduced me to my new family and I went to live with them on the far side of Hungdi's village. But clear as a ray of sunlight that slices through a hazy film I can sense the frozen, dull ache of nothing. I still don't know if I'll ever lose it, the numbness. It's there when I sleep, as I eat, even in my dreams it clings with frigid fingers to my soul. It plagues my thoughts and twists my mind; always it remains, taunting me to forget and to remember – to bring the horror filled night of long ago back into awareness. I hate it, but in some ways it's me. It consumes me, offers me purpose and yet it is ever trying to destroy me.

I don't know how Tonto got me through those years and I doubt I ever will understand why he bothered. But somewhere deep within I think, perhaps, I've begun to feel again. Not like before; the absence of all sensation is still ever present. But I get the impression that something else is growing inside, something foul. I don't want it there, I never have. But it just grips tighter and I can't let it go. It's a part of me, like an extra limb I'm carrying into a fight; it weighs me down and yet it protects me. It keeps me from remembering.

Today I went hunting with Tonto from the back of a horse, firing off several arrows in rapid succession at our quarry while remaining firmly on my mount. I'd nearly tumbled off in the past, but now I finally seem to have perfected the skill the Indians use.

I'm one of them now, a part of their tribe. Most of the children still find me intriguing, and more than half the women think me peculiar as I refuse to wear the hide dresses and have discovered the men's long, buckskin pants and thick jerkins more befitting to me. Tonto considers me incredible. He's said as much; the way I catch onto things so quickly and am able to do whatever he flings at me. I find myself curious at times, but more regularly I detest myself.

Ranger

Kimberly Ranger perished the night I was poisoned, the evening of the murder. I am no longer the governor's daughter; I am simply Kim, or Oginali to many of the others: *Friend*. I found this term strangely grating to my ears for the longest while, but I'm getting used to it. I'm realizing I've become less sensitive to a lot of things, such matters that I would never have dreamed of hearing about, and I'm not just listening anymore, I'm living it.

In certain ways I've learned to live again. I no longer agonize over my old existence every waking hour, though I'll never stop thinking about it. I've come to accept the circumstances — that the now is here and the past is gone and cannot be relived no matter how long I weep into the ground or rage into the darkness. What is purely is. I cannot change it; no one can. I am the cause for all the loss in my past.

Tonto has introduced me to his adopted family, and his aunt was the one who agreed to host me in her home. Though I do believe she holds disapproval for me, what with all the sidelong glances she flings our way whenever I go off with Tonto to the woodlands. She hasn't ever stopped me, but I know she'd dearly like to; I think Tonto has spoken to her on the subject and his words are the only barrier between my freedom and her desire.

The chief is essentially like a grandfather to the entire community, and he has even allowed me privileges to speak at village meetings. I recognize the fact that I ought to feel vastly grateful, but occasionally I just get the idea that I'm a quill in their sides and they put up with me merely to support Tonto.

He's like the brother I nearly had, only older. I still can't shake the image from my mind of the day I first saw him; he looks much more grown-up nowadays. And no matter how notably the other inhabitants seem to only partially accept me, I know he considers me as his own blood sister – as if I had always been there since the beginning. But I can't shake this thought that someday I'll lose him.

I've learned I no longer keep myself breathing for my own reasons anymore; I couldn't even if I wanted to. There's not enough left in me to live on behalf of. I stay alive for Tonto; he needs somebody, and I appear to be the only one he's found. If I perished, he might too. That reminder is the sole thing that keeps me going.

I was presented with a horse as a token of recognition; his name is Heaven-Bound. However, just as the people here don't sit quite right with the idea of me, neither does this animal. He seems tense while I ride him, as if he can sense I was scarred by a creature of demise and now I am one... on the inside.

Months ago, not long after my coming here, Tonto went back to the location of the accident. He saw what was left of the carriage and when he picked through, he discovered a discarded, wooden chest that had been buried in the crash. He found

Ranger

some of the governor's gold and brought it back to me. I kept it, hidden away; why, I'll never fathom. All it symbolizes is the ache, my personal agony. And maybe that's why I hold onto it. I've nearly forgotten what pain is.

My cheek has healed, though it will never be the same as before. The scar I bear is ghastly white and runs from my left ear all the way to the line of my jaw. At times when I grin more than the slightest bit I feel a twinge deep inside it, ever reminding me I have nothing much to smile about.

I don't dare go back to town, not now. Not after the disaster. If I went home, claiming my father's possessions and property as the only existing member of the family, there would be difficulties; no one would recognize me. And I wouldn't want them to. I'm not worth knowing.

The flames burn low in the fire by my side; a young girl and her mother's placid breathing fill my mind, endeavoring to lull my numbness into a thrumming vibration. I fear I will not sleep if I remain here; I must get out. I shall go and sleep in the glade where Tonto found me. I venture there frequently to reflect and to rest. More often than not, Tonto catches me in that place, there not here. I cannot be kept inside these tents for long; I am restless. Always restless. A pull within takes me back, constantly back to the place where I was destroyed. I burn inside, but I am numb.

The stars are cold, the moon is heartless, the wings of the moths and the drone of the bats are loud to my ears. But I will go; I must return continually to that dell. Something about it entices me, and I have not the desire to refuse it. Maybe tomorrow will promise freedom. But what liberty can I gain? I am disheartened. I am broken. And I am numb.

Chapter 4

"If you could learn how to tan pelts as fast as you track game, you'd have the gratitude of quite a few women," Tonto declared, hoisting the trussed-up hares higher on his shoulder.

Kim grunted, her mind wandering far away. She only half-heard what he said. The heavens had clouded over above them, casting the night sky into an even darker haze. Here and there a star blinked through and for brief moments the moon would display its radiant face. But quickly it was concealed once more, plunging the world below into darkness.

Tonto detected her indifference and let the conversation slip into silence, choosing to concentrate on where he set his feet in the dark woodland. Vaulting over a fallen log, he swiftly scanned the area, not particularly fond of being this deep in the woods at twilight. He enjoyed the sites closer to the village such as the glade with the cross, someplace he knew well.

Kim would have been apprehensive about being caught out in the dark woodlands some years ago, now she realized there wasn't much to be concerned with. Nothing roamed these parts anymore that wasn't a natural dweller of the forest except for Tonto and herself. She had been hidden from the creatures of doom there in the Indian village and the beasts would never be able to find her again. She would be forced to live out the remainder of her days in solitude and isolation. But at least no one else would be hurt because of her. She couldn't bring harm to anyone if she was contained here and the creatures weren't able to locate her.

The weak, flickering light of a dozen camp fires shimmered through the thinning trees, beaming out their radiance to greet the hunters. Kim perceived the small forms of children twirling around the stone pits and picked up the sound of their babbling voices all raised together in a humming chant of praise. They leapt and twisted in odd patterns around the circular stone rings, crying loudly or softly as the song rose and fell in cadence.

Tonto hastened his pace as the tipis sprung forward into his vision. The homes he'd always known and cherished and the people who'd shown him kindness when his life had flipped upside-down at a young age swelled his heart.

The pair strolled into the encampment with the rabbits slung across their backs and bows hefted in their hands. They penetrated through the camp to the center and deposited their game beside several women who had been awaiting their return. They would prepare the fresh meat for a meal to be held after the ceremony that evening – Kim was to be properly acknowledged as one of the tribe. Even though she had been granted privileges and freedoms, was presented with a fine stallion and lived with one of the families in the community, she had yet to undergo the ritual that bound her to the clan.

Tonto released his catch. Removing the quiver full of arrows from his shoulder, he settled them beside a hut and frisked away to join the children in their dancing. Kim withdrew her own weapons from her back, setting them with Tonto's, then stepped into the shadows to observe, a stoic expression washing over her strong features.

A petite little girl ran into the midst of the other children. Twirling and giggling, she linked hands with another youth and they spun together, their long black hair flying out behind them. The smaller one broke away and came skipping over to Kim's side. She stared up at the tall female with glossy, inquisitive eyes, tugging on Kim's pant leg. "Co fromas, co'huion." She pleaded, begging the older girl to join their dance.

Kim exhaled pointedly, shaking her head with indifference. Crossing her arms over her chest, she chose to ignore the youth that clutched at her leg in eagerness. The child finally let go when the older girl ceased to pay attention and slunk back to the group of merrymakers.

Presently, Tonto rejoined her near the boundary of the inner circle, his faced flushed from the heat of the fires and the energy of the dance. He elbowed her and dipped his chin toward the children. She flinched away and set her gaze to roam in the opposite direction. She refused to partake in any of this.

Not a single person had asked her if she desired to be a proper part of the tribe. No one had bothered to wonder what her thoughts on the subject were. It wasn't that she didn't care for the people or the village; Kim had a spot in her numb heart for it, but it was a trivial space. They didn't truly believe she belonged, did they? This was purely for display; to honor a custom. Without this ceremony, she wasn't theoretically permitted to live in the community any longer.

Chief Hungdi emerged from the centrally located tipi and marched his measured gait toward the fire ring. The warriors and squaws began to assemble around the pits as well and the children were instructed to end their jubilance and fall into the lines.

Tonto stirred from beside her, taking his place alongside his adopted family and joining hands with his younger siblings. The chief calmed the multitudes with his strong voice as it rang out in the language of the clan. Kim's awareness breezed over his words, not entirely certain what all he was saying, she simply waited for the sentence that would signal her to step into their midst.

The indicated word blazed through her mind and Kim strode forward, the ring of individuals parting to allow her passage through their outer circle. She paced into their group, making her way to stand before Hungdi, her gaze fixed straight ahead. Kim dipped her chin toward him and knelt as she'd been instructed to do. The chief spoke once more, lifting his hands and staff high above his own head and chanting in a sing-song voice.

Kim squirmed; the droning hum grew louder with the added voices of the people repeating back to their chief the customary replies. The warmth of the flames grew intensely searing upon her back and the scent of heavy smoke billowed into the air. Kim lingered there, as if she were being tried and convicted of an offense. The individuals each raised their arms above her head in an arc and commenced their strange melody.

Kim's concentration blurred; her mind couldn't handle it any longer. She pushed to her feet and pressed through the masses, sprinting from the center of the camp and racing into the night. The heat of the fire washed from her body and the pungent odor of smoke gradually left her nostrils. She couldn't take it; she didn't desire this and they couldn't force her to want it.

Kim jogged into the gloomy woodland. Tripping and stumbling through the boughs and over countless broken branches, she staggered back to the dell with the wooden cross. She stalked into the glade, irritation lighting her expression; she allowed the ire to fill her breaths. Kim didn't wish to be in this place either. The hollow held too many memories and limitless horrors.

She could sense the numerous fears and she didn't want to recall them. She had never belonged in the village, she didn't dare return to the settlement, and she hated this clearing and everything it reminded her of.

Kim dropped to her knees near the cross. Hands pressed to her head, she growled at her own stupidity and anger. She hadn't planned to let her fury out but inside the rage fueled her. She didn't know any other way to feel. Anger was the only emotion that was left to her and at times it seemed better to be in wrath then to be in nothing.

Kim sensed an approaching presence behind her. She hurdled to her feet and spun; hands outspread and prepared to defend. She glared hostility into the other being's face. Tonto stood panting on the verge of the glade, his facial features flat. Kim let her palms fall loosely to her sides. The heat from her madness deteriorated; she turned her back. What had he come for? To persuade her to return to the village? Why? What would it prove, what could anyone gain from that?

"Kim." He spoke her name softly, stepping toward her.

"Why are you here?" She snapped, bitterness bubbling into her tone. She couldn't help that her retorts were irate; they merely embodied her only sensation at the moment.

"I could ask the same thing of you." He responded, confused by her bolting from the ceremony. "I don't comprehend what it is that you dislike so greatly about my people. Why do you conduct yourself in this manner?"

She huffed crossly. "You couldn't understand, no one can."

"Not unless you express to me your thoughts. I am at a loss of what to say when I don't even apprehend the problem." He ran a hand through his messy shock of dark hair.

Kim spun to confront him, her eyes flashing with annoyance and regretful wrath. "I am the problem, Tonto! Can't you realize that? I've always been the difficulty, and I will continue to be until the end of my days. There's no point to any of this! Your people loathe me, that is why I cannot be one of them. They despise me nearly as much as I do myself. They simply hide it behind a mask of goodwill." She hung her head and plodded into the tree line.

Tonto trailed her, trying to make logical sense of it all. "Look, Kim," he began, catching her arm. She pulled away but halted her retreat into the forest. "I don't know what the community thinks of you; I cannot see into their hearts. But I do know what is in mine. You are a sister to me and nothing the warriors or squaws can do will sever that. You are my Oginali and I believe that you have a home in the village. Life is certainly not simple, your own least of all. But I beg of you to give it another chance, even if you perceive naught in it for your personal good. I ask that you would come home."

Kim stood panting into the night air, her eyes squeezed tightly shut. The resentment gently began to fade away, and she searched desperately for an alternative emotion to replace it. But none remained; only the numb, aching frozen chill that always held on. "I fear there is nowhere that will ever be my home again." Her whispered words trickled into the evening, the breeze catching hold of them and merging a puffy cloud of white into their midst.

Chapter 5

"Forget not to lead the target; give the shaft time to reach it before your game darts too far out of your range." She had done this countless times before and still he addressed this same exact subject on every hunt. Did he not have confidence in her for this one simple task?

Kim nodded slightly, hardening her gaze and shifting her posture, aiming once again through the brushwood. The arrow felt slippery on the bow's sinewy string as she guided her arm a little further to the right. The smooth, wooden rod gently slackened in her grip, a moment later it was freed and flying, bending across the bow's sleek frame. A small, half smile spread over her lips and Tonto clapped her vigorously on the back. "Excellent!" he exclaimed, bounding over to the lifeless rabbit, a black fletched shaft pinning it the ground. Kim lingered in her stance, the long bow twisting in her hands.

A flash of color flickered through the trees' gangly trunks, catching in Kim's peripheral vision. She swung her head toward the passing shape, identifying the girl bounding their way; Awinita, Tonto's little sister. The youth came crashing into the wooded hollow, her vivid, chestnut eyes wider than Kim had thought humanly possible. Overshadowing the child's features was an expression of penetrating distress. She careened over a fallen stump, crashing into Kim's outstretched arms and wheezed for breath. Tonto was at their side before Awinita could gain her second wind.

"What is the matter?" he asked, searching over her expression with impatient dismay.

Awinita's eyes began to dart back and forth. Her thin, pink lips stirred but either she didn't know how to say what she wanted or her voice was so short of breath she couldn't declare anything more than one word – a name. "Renadear, Renadear!" She cried, reciting it over and over again with feverish gestures directed toward the village.

Tonto shook his head; he didn't understand what her vigorous motions meant. "Come on." He swept her into his stout arms and sprinted from the wood, heading for the camp. Kim was left behind, standing dazed in the emerald light that arched through the dense foliage above.

She cast a sidelong glance over her shoulder at the downed rabbit; it could remain there for the time being. Kim stole her bow from the leafy ground and hurried after the two Indians; something was terribly wrong.

By the time Kim arrived in the village, all the women had clustered together at the edge of the encampment, clutching their little ones close, none of the men , or Tonto and Awinita, were to be seen. Kim broke through the anxious throng and into their midst where a ring of silver haired females huddled around Renadear's squaw. The young wife lay prostrate upon the hard earth, tears streaming down her flushed cheeks. Kim drew one of the older women aside. "Where are the men, Tonto, and his sister?" She glanced quickly at the girl in the dirt. "Where is Renadear?"

The ancient Indian wobbled her head, clicking her beaded braids together. She stared with timeworn, wrinkled eyes and pointed a bronzed, scrawny finger out into the distance – across the fields of grain and the small prairie.

Kim paused for a last evaluation of the exact spot then pushed off toward the location. The sun-worn woman caught Kim's arm as she made to leave. Shaking her head, the grey locks bouncing, she spoke in wavering English. "You no go." Kim pushed the women's bony hand away and leapt into a sprint, a forbidding sensation creeping over a small portion of her being.

The grass rose upward from the earth, high above the prairie's rolling surface, ripping its long leaves against her exposed skin. The thick blades cut at her flesh, but Kim didn't care, she had to find the others. She had to see Renadear; she had to know he was well.

As the meadow passed away beneath her feet, Kim could just make out the petite forms of people standing on the distant horizon. Her thigh muscles seized, but she pushed herself forward, breath catching in her throat and lungs burning with effort.

Tonto and his sister were standing a little way off from the larger cluster of men, at the point where the prairie grass slackened in height. The ridged backs of the warriors met her gaze, but gradually, as she advanced with unrelenting haste, their scattered line thinned so that as she burst forward her sight was uninhibited. By the moccasined feet of several Indians sprawled the prone form of Renadear, or what remained of him. Kim's knees gave out and she collapsed abruptly, a few yards away from where the man had been slain. Her eyes lingered to stare at the carnage even as she ached to look away. Her lungs carried air up to her throat in a yell that surged forth with animalistic and infuriated shock. How? How could this have come to pass?

A hand shot quickly to her cheek and the serpentine scar. It pulsated and burned, mutilating her face into a tormented expression. The monsters had returned to kill yet again. Only this time they had left her a destroyed token of their brutality. They knew where she was.

Kim scarcely realized that she was being hauled to her feet; she could see the sky and the clouds and sense the warmth of the sun beating down on her tortured face, but she could hear nothing.

Tonto frowned directly into her face but she gazed past him. He shook her by the shoulders; she merely rode with his jerks. He shouted her name, but she did not acknowledge a word he uttered. Kim seemed to be as far from reality as the man being borne away to the death platform.

Tonto slipped an arm under Kim's ribs and began hiking her back toward the encampment.

"You should have waited with the women." he grunted beneath his burden, the irritation in his voice finally cutting into Kim's oblivion. She shrank in his grasp but did not pull away; she knew she wouldn't make it walking by herself. Awinita straggled along behind them, her tiny tears lost in the deep grass that nearly engulfed her small body.

They reached the outskirts of the camp, every inhabitant having departed from sight, moving to the inner circle of lodges to light the ceremonial fire of the deceased. Tonto flung back a tent flap and shoved Kim inside the darkened shelter. "Stay here." He spun away, lingering in the entrance for a moment, perhaps contemplating what had occurred. But then he too vanished, the tanned hide rustling back into place, shutting her out from the world once again.

Her head swayed a little, as if it were too heavy for her to hold up alone. The events that had newly transpired weren't supposed to be like this. Loss wasn't supposed to be able to touch her here. This wasn't how it was meant to be.

Kim sat there, numb for hours. No one came for her, and she felt no inclination to search them out. Her mind just kept going over the same thing again and again. How?

* *

The cross brings me no comfort tonight. It is a grave marker, prompting me to remember what has already come to pass and what is bound to occur again. I seem to hold some sort of allurement for these creatures, like a carcass drawing flies. They still hunt me and somehow they know; they tracked me down, and for some obscure reason they want me. Why? What am I to them? Apart from the victim that got away, what makes me special? Nothing. I could tell them that. Anyone could.

After the incident in the village today, I couldn't bring myself to linger nearby once dusk had fallen, I needed to hasten away from all the smoke and death chants. The people's reasoning is flawed. They raise burning remains of rabbits and moan hymns, hoping to bring back their loved one. Even I realize this to be futile. Naught that they do will bring Renadear into this life. He's gone, just like my family.

I slipped out from beneath their vigilant gazes. Tonto regularly says I'm soundless as the shadows, quiet as a mountain lion. I guess he's correct, for no one witnessed my leaving. And even if they had, would they have bothered to come after me? I truly doubt it. Would they have said anything at all? No.

I've tried to forget it, the image of the man's warped and disfigured frame. Was that what would have happened to me if Tonto hadn't been there? Perchance the reason I responded in the manner I did was because I saw myself lying there instead of Renadear. But more than that, I pictured my younger sibling's horrified faces. They hadn't deserved to perish in that fashion, no one did. For what exactly and because of whom had all this happened? Me. I blame myself and rightly so. I know it as truth in my mind but more importantly I discern it with my heart. I am the root cause of my family's passing as well as the young Indian man's.

I've decided to accept this fact wholly, there's naught I can do to repair the past, no way to go back and redeem myself. I'm tainted and I wear the proof of it: my scar.

From here in the glade I can yet overhear the lamenting cries of a grieving wife and devastated village; their pain-filled dirges ride on the breeze and pound into my ears. From here alongside this wooden cross I can still hear the screams of terror from two little children; they flow with the threads of time and invade my mind, accusing me. I cannot change anything; I can't save anyone from the deaths that surely await them. But maybe I can find answers.

My mind has made its choice and nothing and no one will hold me back.

Chapter 6

"Why do you want to go there?!" Tonto exclaimed, his brow creased in perplexity. The mournful anger that had fused into his blood the day before still mixed thickly in his words. He scowled and turned a cold shoulder to fasten a new deer-hide about one of the lodges, covering a gaunt area in the pelt beneath it.

"To find answers." Kim replied bluntly, returning none of the irritation he had flung at her. "I'm sickened and weary of hiding in the dark living for a future that won't be worth anything in the end." Kim extended her hands to assist him in completing the knot he had been fumbling over in his blind indignation.

Tonto pulled away, pinning his firm stare on her face. "And to what purpose would these answers serve?"

Kim beheld him with what she supposed might have been sorrow, if her heart could have felt more deeply of sentiments. "I don't know." She sighed and strode past him to gaze with vacant eyes out into the meadows. "But I'm going. I'm unearthing solutions even if I have to extract them slowly. I need to know what everyone recalls about that night. See if anyone survived, if any of the townspeople saw something. I want to know what these creatures of disaster are. Where did they originate from? And why are they pursuing me?"

Ranger

Tonto's irritation melted away as he listened to her resolve. He exhaled heavily, electing to speak softly. "But to what end, Oginali? I fear you'd learn the truth but it would only drive you further into yourself. I dislike believing you'd be consumed by what you hear. That you'd have no motivation to go on, but I discern it would be so."

Kim spun, her expression blank and features glazed. "I have never had a reason to endure this long." They surveyed each other for a soundless moment, stillness breaching the gap between them.

Tonto's shoulders finally plunged from their rigid position and he lowered his chin. "I know that. But what, Kim, can you do with these facts once you gain them?"

"I have not yet decided. Perhaps I'll return here and linger on in my numbness till the close of my chapter. Maybe, as you say, the reality will force me over the edge. I don't know. I doubt I ever will fathom it until what comes to pass actually transpires." She pushed her feet into the earth, hiking out toward the field where the horses grazed in serenity.

"You would go alone?" Tonto wondered, jogging up beside her.

"You will not be welcome in town; people there don't take kindly to Indians prying about thanks to...Governor Ranger." Kim winced faintly; she'd never told Tonto of her real family. Heaven-Bound lifted his head as she drew near, revealing the whites of his eyes.

"I do not think you will receive a hero's hailing either." Tonto swung up onto the bareback of his paint horse. "I am coming along."

Kim deftly mounted her stallion, dipping her chin in reply. "Very well, it is your choice. But I cannot guarantee your safety."

"To linger in security all one's life and not take certain risks is not to live. Oftentimes you must do that which you fear for the good of another."

Kim grunted, clicking Heaven-Bound into motion. "Do what you want for whatever reason; I'm going merely to find answers for myself." Tonto endured in silence, nudging his own mount into pace beside hers.

Riding, the two wandered a route around the actively awakening village. The Indians would be preparing for a day of grieving. The week of ceremonial mourning had begun. Renadear's squaw had remained awake all the night through, as was custom. She was instructed to abstain from all foods and chant for her lost partner; her body would grow so feeble she'd eventually collapse, thus bringing the period of lamentation to an end.

The riders continued on, prodding their horses into a trot then a canter. They traced the path on through the forest walks and off toward the town. Dark olive foliage burst forth in blooming torrents here and there in between the constant blush of lighter green leaves. Song birds whistled their melodies of acclamation from the tree tops and the horse's hooves generated a muffled, drumming resonance on the dry track. It was strange to think that a place concealing such danger during the hours of darkness could be so serene in the light of day. Or did the creatures strike in the full shine of the sun as well? Kim winced, her thoughts roaming over ideas she didn't wish to consider but couldn't break loose of. What horrors lurked just beyond the immediate, restricted view of the trail? How did individuals go on living ordinary lives when others had been cut from reality so abruptly? Could a mother send her child anyplace without the anxiety that they might be viciously murdered by a wild beast? A warm hand slipped onto her forearm and she lurched, staring at it with creased brow.

Tonto wore a concerned expression. "Are you all right?" he inquired, removing his palm. Kim hadn't realized before that they had arrived at the brink of the woodland and their mounts had slackened the stride to a walk.

"I'm fine," she replied, clenching her jaw and shifting slightly on her stallion's back.

The town was visible in the distance, flaring up against the skyline like a solitary cloud amidst so much empty blue. "I'll be testing the saloon's regulars on their recollections of that night," Kim said, kicking her mount into a faster gait. There were still several lesser meadows to cross between them and their destination. "Where will you be?"

Tonto kept his gaze locked on the horizon, his lips pressed in a tight line. "I don't know. Perhaps I shall call upon the local farrier."

Kim nodded; his proposal was satisfactory. So long as he stayed out of her way she didn't care whom he choose to acquaint himself with. She raised a hand to swipe long auburn hair from her face, her nimble fingers brushing over the rough blemish on her cheek. She'd need to conceal it. A swift visit to the corner mercantile would afford some solution for that. Perhaps she ought to also change her clothing; appearing as an Indian wasn't exactly how one made an impression in a crowd. At least not here, not now.

A short time later, a dark skinned Indian meandered his way toward the farrier's barn and a tall, black-garbed rancher strolled into the saloon. Both desired answers but each with different motives in mind.

Tonto led his brown and white painted horse across the vacant, dirt street and up to the hitching post in front of the farrier's bulky shop; the man and his warehouse also doubled as the town's simple blacksmith for the basic needs of the people. If what Kim had told Tonto was accurate, and from the reaction of the mercantile vendor she was, this would prove be an interesting encounter. Folks here weren't exactly open in their hostility toward Indians, but neither were they pleasant. It was as if someone had forced into the citizen's minds their notion of what Indians were and how one should treat them. Individuals were supposed to accept this ideal rather than coming to their own conclusion of the facts. He would prove that all the opinions were incorrect, if he got the chance.

Tonto strode into the open-doored building with confidence and waited patiently for the man to complete his molding. Hot sparks flew into the air with the rhythmic pounding of the hammer as it beat down on the red-hot section of iron that was slowly taking on a form. With a final swing of his hefty implement, the farrier removed the shoe from the anvil and plunged it into the pail of water near his feet. A moment passed and he drew it out from the cooling liquid, regarding its overall shape. The man laid it down on a flat tabletop with several others that were already finished and reached for another length of metal. Tonto cleared his throat.

The brawny man twisted his gaze toward the sound, his muscles constricting visibly at the sight of the Indian within his workplace. He stared, saying nothing, then swallowed and spoke. "What can I do ya fer?" he inquired, displaying not a lick of anger or surprise in his voice.

Tonto's eyes flicked over him, assessing. "My horse need shoe," he replied in the manner of an unaccustomed English speaker, disordered and hesitant. Better to not throw all his cards out just yet. Let the farrier think he was an illiterate savage for the time being; it might provide an advantage later on.

The fellow's eyebrows rose ever so slightly. "Shall we take a look?"

Tonto nodded, slipping from the stuffy interior into the warm afternoon light. He marched over to his mare, planting a firm hand on her shoulder. "This Agateno or Scout."

"Which shoe is missin'?" the farrier questioned, coming up alongside the Indian and his mount. He rubbed a blackened hand down the mare's back. The man never made eye contact with Tonto, preferring instead to view the horse.

"All," came the simple reply, causing the farrier's hand to falter for a brief instant.

Effortlessly he straddled one of the paint's rear legs and pressed her fetlock, prompting her to pick up that limb so he could inspect the hoof. Standing for a minute or two, the farrier brushed at the dirt around the frog and sole of her foot, finally lowering it to the ground again. "Looks ta me as if her feet are holdin' up fine without no shoes." Straightening, he turned suspicious eyes on Tonto. "This aren't no joke, you're not trying ta chisel me are ya? My time is precious ta me, ya know."

Tonto nodded, flattening a hand on Scout's neck. "My time also valuable to me."

"Then what's the idea, feller? What do ya want?" The man's tone grew sharp with exasperation. "Obviously it's not ta get shoes fer your mount; you don't do near enough ridin' on pebbles 'n rocks ta need 'em."

The dark skinned boy dipped his head in acknowledgement of this fact. "I have questions;

you have answers. I get truthful responses; we both get time back. Agreed?"

The farrier's features pinched together, as if he smelled something foul in the air. "Fair enough," he snorted. "If'n I can give reasonable replies ta yer inquiries with no harm nor damage to my personal life nor business."

"This does not involve you directly. It will simply test your awareness about history – recent history."

"Well, shoot away, mister. I've got things to do and places to be." The man leaned himself up against the hitching post and flexed his jaw back and forth.

Tonto regained his primitive English grammar, launching into his investigation. "September fifth, 1849, you remember that night?"

The man squinted off into the distance, the boot he'd been scuffing through the soil stilled and the dust from the road settled slowly back to earth. His hands had been dangling loosely by his sides; now they curled into tight fists. At last he licked his dry lips and nodded. "Aye, I recall it ; cold as the grave and dark as doomsday. Not much to be remembered."

Tonto would be forced to dig for what he wanted to hear. "But some event that night marked turning point of sorts for your town, that true?"

The farrier absently began kicking at the dirt again. "There might'a been. I can't recollect clearly." He averted his gaze to peer across the desolate street towards the shops and houses further along the filthy road.

"A death perhaps?" the Indian prompted.

The man twisted his neck farther, endeavoring to escape the questions that were quite noticeably making him uneasy.

"Do you recall Ranger family, or did they too slip from your mind?" Tonto probed, his irritation spiked by the man's unwillingness to express things in a straightforward manner and now, to not speak at all.

"Aye." The farrier said, his voice sounding hard and quiet, his face still bowed away. "I remember the Rangers. I can bring to mind the faces of each. I could tell you their names and I can state their preferred places to visit in this town." He turned a hard expression on the Indian, and in that moment Tonto realized just how young the man truly was; perhaps mid-twenties, not much older than himself.

"I can also recall a twilit night's escape, a carriage of riddles, and a driver who never returned to his family." The farrier swallowed stiffly, his glowering eyes boring into the other boy before him. "I know it well, Indian. The night my pappy died it was cold; no wind, no stars, just moon and mist and horrors. There was no goodbye, nothing was told of his journey even to his wife, for his errand was secret. Then he was gone.

"Now you tell me, mister, what part of this has nothing to do with me?" He hurled the sweat rag he had been carrying around his neck into the grime at

Ranger

Tonto's feet. Stalking away, he returned to his shop with taut nerves. The echoing sound of the hammer once again invaded the small world of the blacksmith's shop and the eddying dust kicked back along the path, flying in swirls over the roadway.

Tonto stood there motionless for a while, stunned by the turn of the conversation. In some way, he was certain, the happenings that had taken place that fateful evening had affected every person in this town. And if it hadn't yet, sooner or later it would.

Farther up the street the saloon's double-hinged doors swung wide and a squat, overweight rancher came hurtling out of them. He sprinted to his horse on jelly-like legs, mounted, jerked the animal's head to the south, and galloped off in a haze of sand. A second figure emerged from the tavern, this one tall and dark. Tonto exhaled deeply, observing as Kim straddled her own horse and guided it back in the direction of the village. She hadn't even bothered to see if he yet lingered about. Something terribly wrong had transpired, or something terribly right.

She refused to talk to him that evening, electing to merely skulk off into the shadows of the dying meal fire and sit like a stone. Her rancher's guise was rolled into a wad and tucked away somewhere, but she still had her hat, mangling it between her fingers. Tonto endeavored to share what he'd learned, or hadn't as the situation had

65

turned out sour for him, but she turned a cold shoulder and his words seemed to merely roll over her back and fade into the night, none of it sinking in. He finally gave up, permitting her to have isolation and see if anyone cared. That's what she desired anyway, to be left alone. Fine. He would consent to her terms, at least for now. Tomorrow he expected answers.

Chapter 7

No one can understand the way I feel; I doubt anyone ever will or ever has. Even when I was a child, did my mother know when I needed to be fed or when I wanted to play? Or did she simply guess like everyone else? I sense the world closing in on me, shrinking. Am I real, or a fantasy of my own mind? Did I truly have an average existence previous to this? I can't clearly recall a day of it if I did. There's only room enough in my mind for the hollowness now. Pain wishes to move in as well. So be it. I'm numb anyway. What does more hurt do but add to the frozen sensation? So what?

For some reason I know I'll go back to the town. I discerned that once I'd ridden away from it. I cannot continue to loiter here in this village forever. There's something different about the atmosphere there in town, something familiar. Perhaps if I linger long enough in that place I will become the old me again. But dreams are just that: dreams. They're expectations and desires that our hearts lord over us to antagonize us and threaten us into shifting who we are. I can't change; I'm stuck in this numb, broken body that might as well be dead. I have no right to live, and I can neither see a light nor create one of my own to give me hope. So what is the purpose? To flitter through this lifetime as the walking dead and do no good for anyone including myself? Life is broken, as am I.

I'll go back; I can't help it. Something remote and distant is moving inside of me. I'm not sure I understand it, but it's like a portion of me that perished the night of the accident is being stirred about. Maybe the town holds the key to whatever it is. I shall find it, no matter how hard I have to look. I will search it out, I swear.

"They're back," the hefty man snorted from his spot in the barn's wide doorway. He crossed thick, muscled arms over his broad chest and leaned against the wooden frame.

The farrier glanced up from the man's black stallion and raised an eyebrow. "Who?" he queried, feeling obligated to speak up but quickly re-fixing his mind on hammering the new shoe in place.

"That rancher fella and the Indian." He spat into the dirt, rubbing his boot over the patch of earth. "Not sure what they want, but that one," He gestured a meaty hand toward the foreigner in back, "is nosy. Could get 'imself in a bad way he sticks his nose in where it don't belong once too often."

"Uhmm." The farrier grunted his consent. "The Indian boy was here yester noon, he was asking 'bout things." Completing the shoe fastening, he let the horses hoof slip through his knees to the tightly packed soil. He stretched the kink from his back, coming to stand beside the other man. "Think they're up ta no good?"

The broad shouldered male shifted his bulk and chewed absently at his lip. "Could be. I've never seen that kid around afore, and I hasn't ever seen an Indian in town 'til yesterday." He stirred himself off the door's edge. "Keep my horse here, Jeb, I's gonna go see what all this bosh is about."

"Just don't make trouble if'n there ain't none to begin with," Jeb cautioned, rolling his palms over a sweat cloth. Shaking his head, he turned back to his craft.

"This time, we stay together," Tonto said, tossing Scout's reins over the log hitching post beside Heaven-Bound and binding the tether loosely.

Kim stiffened underneath her concealing attire and her eyes closed in the shade of her wide-brimmed hat. "Fine," she muttered.

Tonto chortled silently to himself; she had an abrasive charm to her. He stepped into stride beside her and they tracked the dust across the street en route for the inn. Their shadows crossed over the doorframe of the ancient, graying house; a third figure trailing close behind.

Kim peered around the dimly lit interior through narrowed eyes; the place smelled musty and dust particles drifted through the air, so heavily in certain places you could disturb it with a hand and the filmy residue would adhere to your skin. The keeper of the inn was nowhere to be seen and judging from the bolts and locks on the rear door, which led further into the dwelling, he wasn't desirous for anyone to come looking for him. Perhaps they shouldn't have troubled with this residence, others might have been more cooperative.

Kim turned, her tolerance setting itself low, and caught the complaining sound of creaking floorboards. A solidly built man stepped out from the gloom, obstructing their exit route. He was no landlord.

Walking with measured strides, he lumbered toward them, halting several feet away. His massive hands swayed casually at his sides and he set his feet, one slightly in front of the other. "Plannin' on stayin' fer a while in Ranger's Valley?" His voice was low and gruff, no warmth of welcome echoed in his words.

Tonto tensed. What manner of trouble was this man looking for?

"We aren't staying long," Kim replied, her own voice deeper than normal. "Just long enough to find what we're searching for." She, too, rooted herself to the spot.

"And what are ye lookin' fer? Perhaps I can shorten yer stay," the man said curtly. Foreigners weren't welcome here.

"Something I doubt you'd know much about," Kim responded starkly, clenching a fist. People here were rather hostile. Had she known that before when she'd actually lived in the town? Had she been like that?

Tonto rested a palm on her shoulder, indicating that she needed to remain composed.

Ranger

"Oh, really now?" the man pursed his lips, sarcasm spilling into his remark. "Somehow I greatly disbelief that, 'specially if this somehtin' has to do with this 'ere town."

Kim put a boot forward, her patience rapidly fleeing. Who was this rabble-rouser anyway to think he knew about her birthplace? She couldn't recall him from earlier in her life, and she never forgot a face. Kim opened her mouth to hiss a comeback, but a tumult of raised voices issuing in from outside caught hold of her attention, and his. "What in the dry-gulch...?" He growled, flicking his head toward the inn's entrance.

Ignoring the arrogant male before her, Kim slipped passed his enormous bulk and glided out the exit. She sprung from the skinny, wooden porch that ran down the length of the shops and business on this end of the street, Tonto on her heels.

An average sized lad with fly-away russet hair bent doubled over in the midst of a growing throng of town's people. Kim sensed her memory stirring. She knew this boy. His father had been an acquaintance of her mother's and he had been her playmate for no small amount of time. But now, would he even recognize her if she got close? Kim doubted it; he probably wouldn't even give her a second look, just like so many others she'd once known.

Kim inched into the outer circle and waited, like the rest of the populace, to see what the youth had run so hard to tell. The boy, Dirk, panted, pushing a rugged hand through his messy shock of hair. "What's up? Who ya need?" many people mumbled in faint voices, some calling out to the lad who had effectively stolen their attention. He held up a hand to quiet them and straightened, gasping in a breath. "Where-where's Jeb?!" He managed to call out, probing through the swarm of faces. "Pa needs 'im! We got wiped out last night. Something done came through the herds, up 'n slew all our cattle 'cept a few who only got hurt bad. Pa wants to try 'n save 'em. I reckon their gonna croak, but he wishes Jeb would come give 'is 'pinion." Dirk divulged, his lungs full once more.

The farrier pushed between the crowded bodies, his fingers wrapped around a yellowing cloth. "I can't do much fer 'em even if they aren't goners, yer pa knows that."

Dirk nodded. "I 'splained it to 'im more'n once; he still thinks it best ye come. Ya know what he's like when he catches on ta a notion. He wouldn'ta even leave the hurt cows; had to send me in his stead. Asides," the lad scuffled his boot into the ground. "If 'n they die too, that's all we's got." He shot a sidelong glance at the older man, his bright sapphire eyes shining. "You got's ta try, Jeb! You just got's ta." His expression was so intense with expectant hope that Kim's heart offered a slight twinge. She dropped her gaze; if only she could support him still, but those days had long since passed.

Ranger

"Aright, son." Jeb sighed, placing a hand on Dirk's slumped shoulder. "Le'me fetch my hat."

"Thank ya, sir!" Dirk cried with sincere appreciation, grasping the farrier's arm with eager gratitude. "Pa'll never forget this!"

Jeb waved the youth off, the two of them trekking to the smith's shop and then on towards the homestead. The cluster of town's folk began to disperse, some to their businesses, others went about their errands, and a few tagged along behind Jeb – maybe eager to add their assistance. Kim and Tonto didn't move as the street emptied out around them.

Her thoughts raced into the past, her mind's eye tracing the path she'd taken a thousand times. Kim began to walk, veering from the road, not following in the footsteps of the others who had just departed for the ranch. Taking the well-trodden footpath meant an hours march; slipping down the more direct route could cut that time in half and guarantee her arriving at the homestead long before Dirk's meager group.

Kim pumped her legs into a jog once she was certain she'd found the old two-track. It had been flushed over with shrubby undergrowth and her boots snapped off the twiggy branches of dry bushes as she sprinted past. Tonto hurried along behind her. Confusion lit his features but he said nothing. They broke into a run and tracked the lane onward into the lengthening daylight.

The ranch's boundary lines came onto view, marked with rotting fence posts that had long since been stripped of their wire. Beyond, the timeworn bleached house and paint-flecked barn rose gradually from the wide-open prairie land. Kim vaguely realized her insides were burning with the exertion, though externally she felt she could race on forever. Her legs flexed like springs, adding to her speed, and her breath came effortlessly. But her stomach turned, her heart throbbing like a drum against her chest, and she didn't know why. Off by the faintly sloping barn, Kim could perceive the petite form of John Bilston, Dirk's father, and several cows splayed out about him. She didn't wish to chance a meeting with him and most definitely didn't want him to recognize her.

Taking a detour that would lead her far around the barnyard, Kim hastened outward toward the pasture land where the remains of the countless butchered livestock were still likely to be. Nearby, she heard Tonto panting from the effort to keep up. She felt him gradually falling behind but her limbs thrust her ever forward and her breath spilled in like she had only just begun to surge. An intense foreboding of what she would discover haunted her innermost mind, but something pushed her on. She had to see, had to know.

In the near distance, the crooked fence line faded into view, set against the paling sky the posts erupted from the grassy turf like thick wooden arms wired together by thin metal strands. All along the enormous enclosure, bodies lay, strewn about near the perimeter as if the cattle had been desperately trying to escape from the pen; almost like something had attacked from within their midst, driving them out towards freedom. But they never made it.

When Kim drew closer, her gut truly twisted, her cheek felt on fire, and her leg muscles started to shudder with spasms. She slumped to her knees on the hoof-shredded soil, her face warping at the sight. Before her, appearing as if they succeeded in breaking down half the fence before their abrupt deaths, hundreds of cows littered the ground. They each seemed to bear mostly the same injuries as the next. Shred and slash marks gouged their way across the cattle's hindquarters. Some had their heads bowed at abnormal angles, others no longer retained their skulls at all. How could someone or something do such damage and harm?

Her eyes glazed over and she stared off into the expanse of nothing. Faintly, her brain registered Tonto approaching from behind. Dimly she acknowledged his cry of shock as he too beheld the slaughter. With purpose, she slowly mounted to her feet. Grasping Tonto by the arm, Kim retraced her tracks with resolute strides. Without a fleeting look back, she strode away, wandering towards the two-track. Tonto squirmed in her grip, turning for a final glance, but her fingers were comparable to iron at that moment and Kim would not allow him to view the bloody scene again.

The creatures had shown their heinous power. They weren't afraid to strike those who were part of her past as well as her present. The hard, mysterious sensation that had started to stir within was breaking loose —her numbness was being challenged. The time to choose was upon her; she had to act or step away. No longer could she lay buried in the obscurity of an Indian village while people were injured and stolen from on account of her. If for no further purpose than that she must put the unnecessary snuffing out of life to rest and do it before something far more precious than cattle was lost. Five individuals had already perished because of her; no more needed to follow. The beasts wouldn't quit until they'd finished her; of that she was convinced.

Tonto's fidgeting succeeded in irritating Kim to the point where she eventually released her hold. "What are you doing?!" he exclaimed, exasperated, vigorously rubbing feeling back into his limb.

Kim spun on her heels, snatching the hat off her clammy head and letting her dark eyes burn into his. She wasn't angry at him, just inflamed against whatever it was that had caused her existence to tumble into pieces and kept her running for years. The moment had come to break free of it. "It's time." Her hands clenched the hat's brim, the miserable article drooping uselessly by her hip. "I'm not secreting myself away anymore. I have to stop and face them or they'll hunt me 'til I die. Who else will be sacrificed before I either give myself up or they let go. And we both know they won't ever leave me be." She turned towards the town, jammed the black, crumpled fabric back on her head, and stalked back the way they'd come.

Tonto watched her go, the weight of her words sinking in. Hesitantly he jogged up beside her, a partial smile forming. "You're going to need to improve your disguise if you don't want folks knowing who you are." Kim nodded, deciding not to look his way. "You'll have to find someone who knows about these creatures so you can be prepared to fight them." She acknowledged his prudent opinion. "And you'll require a partner." She halted, her jaw flexing.

"No, Tonto. No, I'm better off alone." She shook her head. "What if they killed you?" Her eyebrows knit together. "I couldn't watch you die." She winced and kept her gaze fixed on the path ahead.

"Could you watch anyone else breathe their last?" Kim stiffened. Tonto gently strode up behind her, speaking as he came. "Could you stand by observing as some boy gets murdered or a mother cries her last? Are you willing to see another man's livelihood get slaughtered, some pitiable souls survival become crushed? You say you want to end this torture, yet you seem to worry about me. Why? Are you still so immersed in your own agony? Thinking of how you would be angered if I perished rather than how my time had been cut short? No, I believe deep down you yearn to care for others, but the difficulties of your personal problems and trials are all you can reflect on. Your heart needs a change and I'm not leaving until that alteration comes to pass."

Kim shoulders tensed. Then she sighed and let them drop. "Fine."

I don't know how he succeeds in talking me into such things. The bashing he provided of my character was no cause for me to give in to his whims. For some reason my barriers crumbled. Why, I can't contrive. Like so many other aspects of my life, permitting Tonto to join me on my fiery hunt will linger as a mystery for the remainder of time. I don't know where to begin, by what means to contest with these creatures, or even what they are. And who does? One more question I can't answer. But I intend to find out. So I suppose that means I shall have to drag him along with me wherever I go. Just what I need.

My pathetic hat will not suffice as a disguise any longer. It's far too easy for someone to spot my scar beneath its wilting shadow. Though I expect it doesn't matter if anyone sees that now. It may even benefit me, somehow. I've ripped a band of material off my bandanna and slit eye holes through it. The mask is crude looking, but it'll do for the moment. I'll be procuring a different hat to wear over it; this way I'll be more hidden. I suppose everyone will soon recognize that I'm female, too. Oh well. Someday they'd have to know; I reckon now is as decent a time as any. Still, they may not reason me worth their while, a lass in breeches inquiring about monstrous creatures.

The numbness inside me is fighting. Whatever it is that's trying to rise up against my hollowness it's clashing dreadfully with the void of my being. It's an odd sensation. Perhaps it's a portion of my humanity that succeeded in surviving the massacre. Maybe not. Who am I to say? It's a foreign feeling to me. But aren't all emotions abnormal? I'm so used to my detachment from feeling that anything of this sort is out of place. Mayhap it's time to change that, to allow this different sense in and replace the old. Who can tell what this rash idea of mine will do to me. But one way or another I'll wind up changed by the end. For better or for worse.

Chapter 8

"Where would one go to learn about these beasts?" Tonto asked amiably, setting his eyes to wander over the woodland. The morning mist filtered in through the trees, wrapping about their horse's hooves and ghosting along beside them as they rode the well-trodden path.

"Where indeed would one go to be educated on terrible evil?" Kim replied. Guiding her mount with her knees, they skirted a pool of standing water and continued on for a moment in silence.

"How do you find someone who knows much about the habits of wickedness and yet still also understands the means by which to combat it? Somebody who's witnessed the corrupt, comprehends the hateful, but can act on the honorable and fight against overwhelming brutality."

"Riddles and dilemmas without solutions, I do believe we're off to a decent start." Tonto chuckled and clicked Scout ahead on the narrowing trail.

"You're far too jovial to be going on a beast hunt, my friend," Kim returned, raising an eyebrow at his back.

"And you're much too glum." He twisted his upper torso towards her, his entire face beaming. "I haven't beheld this amount of life in you since..." He paused for thought. "Well, never I suppose. Something's stirring in you, Oginali, something that shines through your eyes."

Kim touched her cheek, watching Tonto right his posture, her fingers brushing over the fibrous cloth that veiled the upper portion of her face. If he could see into her, perceiving this faint difference, would others be able to as well? What would they observe therein? A frozen numbness? For a fleeting instant she felt her heart skip a beat and Heaven-Bound stumbled. He quickly caught himself and soon after adjusted his gait. Clenching her jaw, Kim firmed her resolve. Someone had to do this. But could she truly go through with it? Was she strong enough?

"Mayhap we might inquire of the farmer and his son. Perhaps they saw the creatures," Tonto said, persisting with the old conversation. Kim's mind snapped back to reality. He had been speaking for some while but she hadn't heeded it.

"No. They didn't," she stated hastily and more firmly then she'd meant to.

Tonto remained quiet for a minute, gliding with his horse's soft movements, matching her strides with his body's willowy sway. "Then perchance that pleasant fellow we spoke with over to the inn would be eager to add his assistance. He seemed to be acquainted with menace."

Kim snorted, thinking back to the man, conjuring his face in her mind. "I've never seen him before. In all of the past sixteen years that I lived there I not once encountered him. I used to remember everyone I chanced a meeting with, whether it was a long-standing resident of the area or some pleasure seeker stopping by on en route to the city. I could recall expressions and features easily. Names I have not ever been good with, but I don't forget a person's face. Even now, as I can scarcely bring to mind anything from the former days, one such as he would be nigh impossible to forget."

"He may have moved into town after your parting?" Tonto offered nonchalantly.

"Possibly." Kim nodded. "And maybe not." She balled her hand up in her stallion's halter rein, staring out into the forest that swept by them leisurely. "Whichever possibility it is I want to know where he's from, when he arrived, and what his profession is."

"Ha!" Tonto exclaimed, clapping his mare on the rump with vigor. "Perhaps he's the new town undertaker. I'll wager he receives more business than the old one ever did." He chortled under his breath.

"Right." Kim rolled her eyes, brushing the jest aside. "Still, he rubs me the wrong way. People just don't move to Ranger's Valley. It's simply not done. Ever."

"Okay, then," Tonto slowed his mount as the lane broadened out so they could once again amble along side by side. "Perhaps the legend surrounding the settlement drew him in." He shrugged at the momentary thought.

Kim pulled Heaven-Bound up short. "Legend? I've never heard of there being myths about the area."

Tonto and Scout halted a few paces up the trail. He spun in place to look back at her. "Really?" He sounded utterly surprised. "You've not once overheard the squaws chattering about it round the cooking fires or while tanning hides?"

Kim shook her head, prodding her horse into action. "I don't pay overly much attention to anything they say." She mumbled, becoming somewhat more conscious of her former mistakes in the past several years.

"And when you resided in town, not even there did you hear of it? It originated from within that very place, you know."

"No, I don't." She scowled straight ahead, attentively sifting through the few memories she had left of those days, searching for evidence of what he was implying. She'd been a sheltered child growing up in the trivial, dusty settlement. Her parents had not relished living there and eventually her mother had persuaded her father into leaving for a more sophisticated lifestyle in the city — Kim's unexpected engagement had made for the perfect alibi.

In her short existence among the reliable individuals of Ranger's Valley, helping to raise Dirk had been the only *free* thing she'd been allowed to assist in. Every other moment had someone continuously picking at her, fussing and protecting. She'd never understood why.

Tonto voice seized her attention and weaved for her a walkway into the past. "Legend says that Ranger's Valley was once governed over by a bloodthirsty man, Vukodlak, who required of the townspeople unfaltering servitude unto him or something worse than death would come upon them should they refuse. The story goes on: a man arose with the desire to quell the wickedness and to confront the dreadful master of the town. The man was Vukodlak's brother.

"It says that as the siblings fought their great battle in the midst of the town, it was difficult to make out what went on as their encounter was intense. But finally, the brother conquered over Vukodlak and cast him out of Ranger's Valley along with all who had willing followed him. The brother then went on to liberate those who had been harmed, abused, and bound under spell during the rule of Vukodlak. He swore them each to secrecy.

"The man set up a new governor, one who had also been vowed to silence. Shortly after, the brother vanished. The lore said that he soon died of the wounds Vukodlak had given him in the fight for he was never seen again. But it also states that he had an heir, a child that, when he perished, was hidden in one of the people's own households in the settlement of Ranger's Valley.

"Vukodlak still exists. His masses of underlings have grown and he progresses in power every time a new supporter joins his ranks. Legend says that when Vukodlak comes back for his revenge, the child of his brother will rise up and defend the town. He will fling Vukodlak into such a place wherefrom he will not ever return and he shall bring to an end all who still follow the fiend." Tonto shrugged, breaking the bond to the fable world and its mysteries. "But it's just a myth."

Kim rode in silence for some time, the whitened buildings and shops escalating into view and drawing ever nearer. "Everyone has heard this legend, you say?" she inquired, as the forest fell away behind them.

"Indeed, we tell it to the children and threaten the naughty ones that Vukodlak will come for them if they don't behave. I'm sure you must have caught it being mumbled around."

She undoubtedly had, though didn't comprehend its significance and hadn't cared to either. "Possibly, though I've never taken it to head or bothered to absorb its meanings." Kim mused. "For some mysterious reason my parents didn't wish me to know of this folklore. It seems they went to certain pains to keep me from this account and any other there may have been. Why? What harm could it do? What where they hiding? Some darker secret, perhaps?" Her mind reeled with the possibilities. "What of this Vukodlak's followers? What form did they take?"

"You're not actually suggesting this fable is true on any accounts?" Tonto raised his eyebrows and his dark complexion clouded over with the thought.

"I pray it's not." Kim urged her stallion into a canter, pulling out in front of Tonto and breezing into town. What sort of welcome would they encounter today? Not a pleasant one. That was almost assured.

"She's just asking fer trouble." The stalky, well-built man said, clenching a fist. He glared out from the business's grimy front window, leaning forward with his eyes narrowed.

The mercantile owner barely glanced up from the account books, his eyes flitting over the Indian and masked stranger who had been observed riding into the town for the past couple of days. He repositioned his charcoal stub and resumed his work with the sums and figures in the open ledger.

The giant herdsman hauled himself up, pulling away from the wooden framed viewing space. "Put that under my account." He said hooking a finger over his shoulder at the paraphernalia on the countertop. "I'll be back fer it later."

The supplier dipped his head in agreement, keeping his attention fixed securely on the entries before him. He thought it healthier to stay ignorant of other men's dealings so as to remain innocent if anything was to happen. And what if he had supplied the farmhand clothes for the Indian lass, who clearly wasn't an Indian? He had simply been looking out for his interests.

The immense man's lip twitched. Springing off the outer porch that attached to the general store, he sauntered across the street toward the hitching post where the two had tied up. Strolling in a deliberate arc around their mounts, he appeared to be speculating their worth before coming to a halt between both horse's heads. "Now ain't I seen you two afore?" he questioned, the sarcasm thickly layered in his words. He flexed his biceps and crossed them almost too casually over his wide chest.

"Yes," Kim retorted hollowly. She didn't consider him worthy enough to receive a *sir* on the end.

"We're searching for a storyteller." Tonto broke in before the enmity grew anymore. Already he could have split it with a knife. "You don't happen to know where we could find one, do you?"

The rancher shrouded his astonishment of the Indians ability to communicate in such a fashion, choosing to rivet black intimidating eyes on the dark skinned boy. "I might." He shifted his incredible mass into a less-tense position. Kim's face twitched. "Depends on who yer looking fer and why."

"Oh, any riddle weaver will do. Perhaps a learner of legends, one of those well-read individuals you sophisticated folk ogle over." Tonto shrugged, his speech more like a cultured gentleman than an illiterate.

The man observed him for a minute, hesitating before speaking his understanding on the subject. "The bestest knowledgeable man we have in this here town's the minister. 'E knows 'is history, if that's what yer after: the past."

Kim felt the incurable urge to clarify just how much she'd prefer to leave all former years where they belonged, but perhaps the preacher could assist them. He was, after all, well aquatinted with the reality of evil and knew how to challenge it. "We're looking for him exactly. You wouldn't by chance be aquatinted with the place where he resides, would you?" She questioned, endeavoring to restrain her contempt. Something about this man rankled her – his stature, his manner, or was it his atmosphere? Her face seized up again and she rubbed at the fibrous mask.

The man screwed up his features in disgust and scowled down at her from under thick brows. "I would *happen* ta know where 'e is." And although Kim was tall, he loomed.

"Would you be so kind as to show us?" Tonto casually stepped between them, almost positive they'd go to blows if some solid object did not deter them.

The ranch hand heaved a deep breath, refocusing. "Why? You plannnin' on convertin', Indian?" This statement produced a hearty chuckle from only one of the party.

Tonto and Kim remained ridged, neither seemed to blink an eye or even exhale a breath. The man's facial muscles went slack. He grunted, pushing off the tethering pole and beckoning them behind him with a flick of his hand. "Follow me." He scuffled off across the filthy road, kicking up a sooty cloud in his wake.

Tonto offered Kim a casual shrug, gave Scout a finale pat on the neck, and proceeded to take lengthy strides in order to catch up with their guide.

Kim flinched as the blood rushed to her face and head; an overwhelming sense of lightheadedness caught her off guard and she latched onto the hitching post for support. She blinked several times, her vision fading to black for a moment. But then everything returned to normal in the twinkle of an instant. Kim swallowed and took several tentative steps after them, anticipating the overpowering tides return. It didn't resurface.

"I'll warn ya, he gots some bizarre thinkings." The giant fellow pressed the door of the timeworn chapel inwards, staying to one side. "Don't let 'im offended ya none." He sneered and sauntered off down the street, arrogance in his haughty gait.

The church was properly sized for the small western settlement it was designed for. Rows of crude, wooden pews lined the isle way. At the head of the building a humble podium, with a simple black-covered Bible resting upon it, stood erect and a few low tables held high-reaching candles that flickered in the breeze of their passing. It was dank and faintly chilly in the uncluttered sanctuary causing Kim to shiver, her spine tingling. You could feel the echoing presence of the place; if one were to sneeze at the far end someone on the opposite side would be able to perceive it as if the individual had coughed beside them.

Tonto rapped lightly on the flaking door that was embedded into the side of the chapel's outer room. When there was no reply, he twisted the wooden knob and pushed into the chamber. The interior was warm, though not stuffy, and sunlight poured in from a large open window. A cluttered writing desk, high-backed chair, and a low-lying table were assembled along the far wall. Books lay everywhere; spread over the carpeted floor, on and around the furniture, as well as in the hands of a young male who appeared reasonably stunned by their unexpected entrance.

Kim scuffled her booted feet. Bursting into this man's study, outfitted as they were, most likely wasn't the proper way to initiate friendly relations. He probably thought it was a raid.

"Can I be of service to you?" His voice drifted across the trivial space between them and he gently lowered the manuscript he'd been pouring through to the table near his knees.

Tonto strode further in, Kim on his heels. "I trust that you can. We believe that you ought to be capable of answering several of our gripping questions."

A generous smile emerged on the man's handsome face. "Well, I'm certainly willing to try at least. Depending on the query I may not be able to provide you with a very easy response, but I shall endeavor to do my best." He took in both his visitors with genuine welcome illuminating his features, making him the only sincerely pleasant person Kim had encountered here abouts thus far. "I can't say that I venture to recall having seen your faces afore. Though, I haven't been in town for but a short while."

"What ever happened to Reverend Maximus?" Kim inquired, regretting the words only after she'd finished them. The reverend had been the church's minister throughout her short span of time here. That was years ago now and no one needed to realize that she knew the recent history of the settlement and its inhabitants.

The chaplain observed her with an attentive eye; something about her fascinated his curiosity. "He grew ill and was conveyed to the city in the North where they could treat his condition. I was sent to continue the holy work in his stead." Watching her carefully, he tried to judge her reaction.

Kim refused to meet his penetrating gaze, choosing to peer instead at the volumes by her feet. "Did you know him?" he asked quietly.

Tonto leapt in, saving Kim from following the conversation to a place neither wanted her to go. "My name is Tonto and this is Kim. We came seeking solutions, not additional questions."

"Of course." The man beamed an apologetic smile in their direction. "And I am called William.

Please, do come in. It's not much, but I consider it home." He waved them further into the disordered compartment.

"Thank you," Kim succeeded in croaking out. This William managed to place her nerves on edge, though in a different fashion than the arrogant rancher had.

Will relocated various loads of books to the already-occupied desk, revealing a wobbly-legged stool and another chair. He presented them to his guests, a hand breezing through his ruffled blond hair. "Apologies for the chaos. I don't regularly have visitors. I'm still working on my organizational habits." He cocked a half grin and chuckled. "Now, what can I assist you with, friends?"

Tonto elevated an eyebrow at the term but lingered in silence. This was Kim's plan; she could take the initiative. She cleared her throat and towed the replacement hat off her tousled brown head, running the durable material over her palms.

"We're looking for someone," She began. "But first we require information." She scowled into her lap; this wasn't going in the right direction. Masking their intentions would only lead to more confusion. Perhaps she should simply express her suspicions and in turn he might provide her with straightforward replies.

Fetching her eyes up to meet William's, Kim restarted with what she had meant to say in the first place. "Do you know the legend of this town and of Vukodlak?"

Will pursed his lips and presented a partial shrug, casting his gaze between the two. "I've heard it before, naturally. It's fairly frequently mentioned in the northern cities, rather a traditional sort of myth it seems. In fact," Will said, his face brightening further. "Reverend Maximus recited it to me afore I journeyed here." He smiled and laughed again. "Yes, he believed I ought to achieve a relatively decent understanding of the history in this place and the folklore of its inhabitance. Quite a fascinating account if you ask me."

"Undeniably." Tonto nodded, uncertain as to why Kim had brought the lore up at all.

Will crossed his arms over his chest, regarding them both — one twirling her hat in circles, the other glancing about the apartment. He chortled internally and raised his eyebrows. What were an Indian and a masked lassie doing in his abode? He smirked, finding it rather humorous to catch himself in this situation.

"Did you know Dirk, the young lad who was into town yester evening?" Kim inquired, taking time to work through her odd sequence of thoughts.

Will bobbed his head, his expression solemn all at once. "A horrible tragedy for him and his father. I witnessed the devastation and I can't fathom what sort of existing animal could do what these atrocious creatures did to the unfortunate man's cattle."

"I know..." Kim stared out the window, lost in a memory that led her far away from the small side chamber in the church.

"You saw them, as well? The livestock I mean?" William's brow puckered.

"We have an indication of what produced such loss." Tonto interjected, grasping hold of Kim's idea. "We were also hopeful that you would be able to aid us in determining several details about these beings."

Will smiled apologetically at the Indian. "Well, friend, I'm afraid I'll not be much help. It sounds to me as if you already have a far better idea of these creatures then I. But," He loosened his arms and shrugged. "You're welcome to ask anyhow; perhaps I can offer some type of advice." Will paused, glancing at the ceiling with a smirk. "I can't promise it will be useful, however." Tonto grinned. He liked this man.

Standing, Tonto relaxed against the door frame in a comfortable position. "Maybe you can tell us if the rancher and his son observed anything irregular previous to their cattle being slaughtered."

"I could enlighten you as to that point, but I doubt it would benefit you in locating these creatures. They are what you're searching for, are they not?" He had deduced their intent, though a number of things still remained a mystery. Like the female. Who was she? Why did she wear the mask? What did she have to hide?

Kim rose from her chair, following Tonto's example. "Yes." She stared him straight in the eye and her voice spoke resolve. "We mean to hunt them."

"If you don't mind my curiosity, why?" Will asked, convinced there was more to it. "They're extremely lethal it would seem."

"Isn't that reason enough? They slay for amusement and deprive the earth of all things honorable and breathing. That ought to be sufficient motivation for any man." Kim fervently declared. "We need help though." She persisted, not waiting for his response. "We don't yet know in what way to pursue them or where to look. I'm not even sure what nature of beings they are." She peered passed the minister and out the large window once more. People hastened across the filthy street; up and down the broad porches that connected the business and houses they roamed. Chancing upon an acquaintance, they'd pause along their route to exchange gossip and then hurry on their way. All of it, all of them, so utterly vulnerable. They needed a protector who could stand as a vigilant guard.

Will took a deep breath, sighing it out gently. "I'm not sure what I can do. I've heard numerous stories and plenty of them recount a sort of beast that destroys characters heartlessly. But they're all merely fables. A vast portion of them are most like your own legend here, in fact."

Kim's countenance remained stoic. She glanced sideways at Tonto, keen to observe his reaction. Will spun his emerald eyes, perceiving the noteworthy stare she'd given her Indian counterpart. "Hold up." He straightened. "You don't actually believe the tales and folklores are truth? That's ridiculous. They are purely used with the intention of presenting a lesson, nothing more."

"Certainly that *was* their purpose," Kim agreed. "But what if their instruction was teaching us how to fight? To challenge the foul things that truly are out there. What if," She stepped a pace towards him, minimizing the distance betwixt them. "What if they're simply history passed down through the ages? What if they're the past put into stories so even the youth could recall them painlessly?"

He stared at the unusual woman before him, his forehead creasing deeply. Although he couldn't distinguish her entire face for the black guise that shrouded it, the intensity of her avid eyes spoke volumes; she wasn't joking. Will swallowed. W*hat if she was correct?*

"You seem to be a very pleasant and rational man," She said, traipsing a path through the book-scattered floor to Tonto's side. "Please, tell us what you know."

Will hesitated for but a moment more. "Alright, I'll explain the fables I can yet remember." He pushed a pathway toward his writing desk, leaving a hand to tarry on the smooth surface as he turned.

Ranger

"The legend that most closely describes and contains each of the others I've heard, including yours, arose from the journal of a Latin reading man who stumbled upon the tale as he was sifting through his deceased grandfather's documents. And, if I can recall it accurately, it started with two children, brothers of noble blood. They existed in a time where empires had yet to be built and boundaries still to be established. Their father, through much sweat and taming of wildernesses, constructed a kingdom; grander, some say, then any that has been or will be. The two siblings, when they were of age, were to rule over the land their father had conquered for them, together.

"Days lapsed into years, and the ages took their toll upon each of the brothers. One matured in honor and courage, hailed by the people as a noble champion. But the other grew jealous; he had also completed acts of boldness, just as his brother had and yet no one acclaimed him. He fell away from the kingdom and delved into the dark arts: sorcery, witchcraft. He advanced in power and presently had scourged and occupied a land that once was under his brother's vigilant protection.

"The corrupt brother, who your account names as Vukodlak, assembled those who were devoted to him and granted them powers: abilities to shift in form beneath the rays of a shining moon and a thirst for blood that he poured into their veins. He fixed a spell over his followers, to safeguard them from harm. And he spoke into their minds so as to drive their will that they might serve him alone.

"Most accounts go on to say that the kingdom brother set out with an army to take back the domain his malevolent twin had seized and to vindicate the peoples who suffered under the harsh law of Vukodlak. The conflict persisted long and the fighting was fierce, but only those who rallied beneath the banner of the kingdom lost their lives. For at first, none could wound the body changers, the enchantment of protection was far too great for any of the weapons to penetrate.

"As the story goes, an old man who had joined in the forces of the realm defender was wandering further into the desert, searching for a spring of fresh water in the dry and thirsty land. He staggered into a quarry, a pit of rock that had once been a silver mine, and realized he had become lost. He roamed for hours, trudging in circles as the high sun gradually sank to the horizon's rim. Yet he could not even rediscover the path he'd taken into the mines.

"Overhead a cold, orange moon rose and from somewhere behind him in the echoing quarry trenches, he perceived a noise. A figure shifter had trailed him into the mine and now, as the night pulled its blanket of silence over the world, had come to finish the soldier. Swinging about, the timeworn man swept what appeared to be a knife blade from the chalky ground. Brandishing the weapon, he turned to confront his foe. The man knew nothing could kill it but he was not about to perish without a fight. So he hefted the thin knife in his calloused palm and paused, waiting for the creature to leap. As it sailed through the air towards him, he dropped to his knees and thrust the blade up into its gut. The beast yelped like a pup and writhed away from the soldier. The man surveyed the scene in absolute shock as the shape changer thrashed about on the rocky ground and then fell dead.

"The man removed the knife from the carcass and, shortly after, the being melted into ash before his eyes. Sprinting through the quarry, he eventually found his way back to the encampment of the kingdom brother. In the soft light of the lanterns they discovered the blade he had employed as a weapon was actually a sliver of hardened silver.

"With this new discovery the battle began to turn ill for Vukodlak and he became enraged that his enemies had found the one feebleness in his warriors. He cast yet another dark magic over his followers, one that permitted them to alter their form at whichever time they chose; no longer did they have to delay till twilight to be the blood-sick ravenous beasts and neither did they have to linger in that form if they elected not to. With this improved outlook, Vukodlak directed them to hide amongst the groups of soldiers that belonged to his brother. From within they wreaked ultimate havoc, for you could not discern who was an opponent until it was far too late.

"The story continues: back and forth they fought, either side nearly winning. Finally the kingdom brother declared that no more blood should be split, and he avowed to fight Vukodlak himself, brother to brother. Whosoever won the match would be the victor of the land. And, as you know, Vukodlak was vanquished. The remainder of the tale is essentially the equal to your own. Vukodlak was not killed, only cast out. The child of the kingdom brother was given to the new master of the land Vukodlak had occupied, and this decedent will rise to the task of opposing Vukodlak in one finale encounter and save us all. So on and so forth." Will waved his hand in a circular motion. "There are different renditions, though they all follow the identical plotline to some degree."

"So, these beasts were slain with silver." Tonto mused, rubbing his chin.

"They also say," Will strolled back toward them, his thumbs latched to his belt. "That if you get injured in any way dreadful things happen to you."

Kim and Tonto shared a significant look.

"The myths say if you survive you'll become distorted and misshapen or worse: you'll carry a portion of their curse within your innermost being and if you nurture the wrong feelings, you could become one of them." Will bent at the waist to retrieve a book. "But, again, those are just additional fables. No one has ever lived to describe being attacked by our cattle slaying creatures or by the mythological animals in the story. Isn't that what you seem to believe? That they are one in the same?"

"I don't just believe it," Kim whispered, rubbing a finger over the pale, raised flesh on her cheek. "I know it."

Chapter 9

"I would not venture outdoors for long," Kim cautioned William. The two stood on the chapel's open porch, Tonto was trotting in their direction leading Heaven-Bound behind his mount. "I do believe a storm is on its way."

"What form does this tempest take?" Will inquired, glancing sideway at her.

Kim drew her black rawhide gloves snug about her arms, rolling her shirt sleeves over them. "It hides behind the guise of a fairytale but destruction and death are its companions." She said cryptically, regarding him with all seriousness. "If I'm not mistaken, you shall be their next target."

He huffed good naturedly. "Who would want to harm me? What have I done?"

Tonto reined Scout in. The stallion trailing behind jerked its head, coming to a standstill. Kim clomped down into the street, taking her horse by the halter harness. The animal seemed particularly skittish about his rider at that moment, dancing backward as she mounted. "You supplied me with information; you've essentially marked yourself as an objective to be dealt with. Just be wary." She warned. Too many people, who'd either been close to her as a child or had aided her recently, were carrying the burden of her actions. They didn't need another casualty.

"Come on, Kim." Tonto called from further up the road, beckoning her to follow.

Ranger

"I'll see if I can't find anything more about these creatures." Will offered, shrugging. "Perhaps some of the town's folk know a thing a two." Kim expression morphed into annoyed confusion.

"Don't worry," He held up a hand to stay the river of words she was surely preparing. "My God safeguards me. Naught can happen outside of His will. And besides, I'm intrigued."

"Nice of him to offer us service." Tonto mused casually. The town shrunk away behind them, lost to the folds of dry, rock-strewn desert and shrubby cacti.

"He's a fool." Kim scowled, her gaze locked on the hazy, heat-waved horizon.

"Maybe." Tonto agreed, allowing for a brief hush before he changed the topic. "Where is this mine, anyhow?"

Kim's disposition altered promptly, her words carrying the zealous tang of adventure. "If what Andrew told me when I was a child is true, then it ought to be out there." She pointed off into the empty distance where the showers of humid sunlight undulated on the air. "South of the settlement, that's what he'd always say: "South 'til you've nearly run back into the north again." So, we just keep riding until we can see it. I suppose it was reasonably far off, though he never could sneak me away long enough to take me there. Someone was always watching." Kim rolled her shining eyes. The barber as well as chef for the governor's household,

"old" Andrew, constantly had fascinating stories to tell her as a youth.

"And it's abandoned, you say?" He probed, squinting into the bright sunshine.

"That's how Andrew put it: "Vacant as a grave, dark as the night, and dusty like a bowl of dirt. Nobody ventures to it anymore because they've forgotten what it's there for."" Heaven-Bound plodded over the clay and rocks underneath his hooves in an uneven gait, jostling his rider.

"Do you think the quarry in Will's legend is at all similar to this one out here? I mean, what are the chances that every settlement within miles each possesses a story akin to the one from Ranger's Valley? How ancient that parable must be to have journeyed so greatly." Tonto whistled with the thought.

"Maybe it's not so old after all." Kim contemplated, her expression still and watchful. "What if it occurred in our lifetime? Could it be our parent's story, our grandparent's account? Did they live what we're only hearing about?"

"I doubt we'll ever know." Tonto shook his head. "But we each have our own individual stories to live though, all slightly different. Some people's narratives are written down, others are passed on in histories from generation to generation, and still others will never be recognized for their noble deeds. And perhaps it's those that ne'er get told – the ones about individuals who fought the invisible battles, who mastered mountains and danced with the waters — maybe it's them which are of most importance. Perhaps we are of that rank and no one will ever understand our journey. But we'll fight our hardest; we'll do our finest because it will matter, at least to us."

Kim rode on in silence. The sun torpedoed past overhead. Noon flowed away and gradually the heat began to subside with the sinking of the brilliant orb's bright face. Ahead, a dusky shadow emerged, a cavernous hole ripping a path through the earth. Kim pulled her stallion up short and stared keenly into the pitfall, portions of the darkness peeling back as she drew nearer.

"The mine?" Tonto asked, his words half swallowed by the evening air.

Kim nodded, clicking to Heaven-Bound, and urging him forward. But the stubborn animal refused to budge one more step. Weary of dealing with his unyielding behaviors, Kim dismounted and dropped the reins to the gritty dirt. "Stay." She muttered, turning a cold shoulder.

Tonto ground tied Scout alongside the stallion and the two strode toward the edge of the first pit-drop into the mine, peering down into the rocky quarry. A dim radiance still spilled over the skyline, illuminating certain crevices below in rosy light. The initial precipice was the sharpest in descent, dropping into a plummet of roughly seven feet. It leveled out fairly smoothly and only plunged gradually in short steps after that. Great, dark caverns stared out at them like hollow eye sockets in the side of the hill. Browns, reds, and yellows mixed together forming the different rock types, and here and there a shining fleck imbedded in the stone would catch the light. "Keep a sharp eye, snakes like shaded crevices." Kim advised, lowering herself to sit at the very brink.

"You're just going to jump down there?" Tonto's eyebrows leapt high in disbelief.

She nodded, shooting an unseen glance his way. "You can attempt to find the actual route the miners would have constructed, then you can lead the horses down."

He cast a momentary, nervous look over the edge. "I believe I shall do that."

"Afraid of heights?" She asked, chuckling to herself. Kim scooted her thighs over the ledge and twisted around so that her stomach was where her rear had been. Gripping the jagged edge with her hands, Kim let her feet dangle down toward the quarry floor. She relaxed her hold and bent her knees as she landed to absorb the impact of the slight fall.

Kim brushed her palms off on her pant legs and swept her gaze along the rocky perimeter. Removing the hat from her head, she shoved it under her belt. A rattling sound echoed off the quarry walls, but the source of the noise must have been further up the ravine, for she saw no movement in the immediate area.

Kim swiped a loose strand of lighter colored hair from her forehead and traced the upper ridge with her eyes, wondering if Tonto would discover an alternative path into the mines. Beyond a massive boulder that obscured a portion of the gulch, she caught sight of a distorted silhouette that appeared to nearly be glowing. Did silver spark in the moonlight? Cocking her head to one side, she scrabbled over the loose pebbles and scampered through the soil toward an open expanse where a clear view would avail her.

Skirting a mound of hewn stones, she could almost see all the way down into the ongoing, man-made canyon. The silver-encrusted slate twinkled with the turning of the moon and the caverns empty mouths scowled ominously in the darkness that was rapidly approaching. Kim froze as she came into the clear, her eyes widening and her lips parting in silent wonder.

Below her, in one of the lower ditches, shining against the evening-scape and white as milky silk, a stallion of elegant beauty loped. He snorted and in the descending chill the breaths appeared as smoke billowing into the frosty air. His ears lay back, listening, and his fluid tail was held slightly erect. He pranced back and forth, anxiously searching for a lane of escape from this land of rubble and rock.

Kim looked on, captivated by this animal that was more graceful than any deer. How had he stumbled into the quarry to begin with? She was curious, as well as fascinated, and slowly began to shift her way ever nearer.

Above on the canyon's rim, Tonto sought for the gradual slopping walkway used to convey of pack-mules in and out of the mines. A flash of white streaked passed his vision, and he swiftly swung his head to catch sight of it again. Far below his location, in the deepest section of the excavated pit, a horse the color of pure snow jogged in circles; at times it would rise onto its hind feet, lashing at the air. Abruptly the stallion turned, his mane swirling in the frosty evening breeze, and cantered back up the inclined rock toward the broader, exposed area.

Tonto's cry caught in his throat and he gagged. Charging horses were dangerous but standing in their path, nay! Not just standing, but hiking closer was even worse. And that was exactly the sort of scene Tonto beheld beneath him. He tried calling to Kim, hoping she'd dive out of harm's way in time, but his voice was weak with distress. He couldn't manage anything more than an insignificant yelp. Acting on instinct rather than thought, he dropped to his rear and slid off the lofty ledge, plummeting into the quarry pits below.

His legs crumpled underneath him but he caught himself with his hands and knees. Rising as swiftly as his body would allow, Tonto sprinted headlong up the ravine.

Rounding the bend, he froze stiff in his tracks and blinked several times. Ahead of him, as the moon mounted overhead, Kim stood with a hand resting on the muzzle of the white stallion. The horse held perfectly still, gazing at her with its liquid black eyes. Tonto's shoulders slumped as he exhaled a sigh of relief and grimaced when the sting in his knees finally registered with his brain.

The animal bowed its long, pale face toward him and Kim followed suit a heart-beat later. She offered a slight smile. "Find a path down?"

"Yeah," he nodded, straightening to peer about. "It's a little tough on the knees and scrapes up the palms a bit, but all in all I think it's safe to say the drop was steeper than the one you took." He displayed his teeth, flashing in stark contrast with his darker skin.

"Precisely what you had in mind, right?" She rolled her eyes, stepping to the side, a hand on the horse's sleek neck.

Tonto perceived the small spark that had lighted in his partner. Something was shifting. "Where'd he come from?" Tonto wondered, gesturing at the snorting steed.

"I don't know." Kim replied, returning her attention to the animal beside her. "It appears as if he can't even decide how he got here. But somehow he must have discovered the seemingly elusive pathway the mineworkers would have used. I highly doubt he leapt into this pit."

"Right." Tonto agreed. His thumbs found the raw-hide belt about his waist and he hooked them through.

Kim slid her palm off the stallion and marched a few paces forward. "I suppose we should do what we came to do." She cast a sidelong glance at her companion and trooped to the entrance of a gapping cave, the horse trailing her footsteps.

Kim strode into the gloomy cavern's mouth, endeavoring to adjust her eyes to the dim light so she could penetrate the unwelcoming darkness. Her boot knocked into some solid object and it rolled across the stony, uneven floor with a resounding metallic clatter. "Tonto," She whispered into the murk. "Did you bring your flint and steel?"

A low crack and a flash was her reply. "Have something for me to burn?"

"Can you provide some extra sparks? I may have an object for you to light." She said, peering hard into the emptiness.

"Sure..." His voice trickled off as he scraped the two fire-starters together. Tiny waves of brilliant luminance exploded, pushing the shadows away for several meager seconds.

Kim rapidly swept her stare about, catching sight of the device she'd kicked. Hustling over to it, she bent double and pried the rusty handle from the slanting bend it had been affixed in. She fetched the item for Tonto, presenting it to him with a shrug. "Possibly you could set the kerosene in this ablaze, if there's still a sufficient amount. Who can tell how long it's been sitting here in disuse."

Tonto accepted the timeworn, tarnished lantern from her and, tearing a small strip of fabric from the hem of his shirt, lit the cloth. He swiftly shoved the flaming material down the lantern's open neck toward the area of the wick. His flame dwindled and nearly went out, but the ancient textile cord inside attracted the heat and in a moment ignited with a flash. "Your lamp." He said, presenting the light to Kim with a flourish.

Using the lantern to illuminate the grimy cave, she gazed about. The ceiling wasn't much higher than her head and the stony slate melded the different hues of crimson, russet, and some olive tones. The cleft had evidently been blasted out of the rock with detonating powder, for the sides and walls were jagged and cutting in places; man-made tool marks marred other sites where boulders had been removed and left behind scooping holes. Various midsized rocks sat scattered across the ground and all along the bottom perimeter, and encasing the dirt in a glittery sheen, lay silver dust. Kim bowed her back and rubbed a trifling amount between her fingers.

Traipsing deeper into the cave, Kim could see veins of the precious metal running through the walls, dancing in zigzag patterns along the stone. "It would take forever to harvest this, at least if you needed anything of significant quantities." She muttered, ducking under a low overhang.

"There must have been a larger deposit somewhere," Tonto decided, following close behind the light bearer. "Otherwise they wouldn't have wasted the time blasting out these caverns unless they reckoned there was additional silver further in."

"Yes but if there was a vast measure of it around here, why'd the miners abandon it?" Kim tested, pushing the lamp before her as a guide.

Tonto lingered in silent contemplation. Perhaps something had scared them off, or a cave-in had cost them too many lives. "Tell me," He brushed a spider's adhesive webbing from his face, "from here, even if we discover a silver spring, as it were, how do you hope to proceed?"

"With more questions, most likely." Kim responded, flicking her light off the shiny metal.

"Sounds like a tentative plan." Tonto nodded, inhaling a deep breath. He had gotten himself saddled with this and it was his fault alone.

Kim saw the conclusion of the cave from where she stood and no heaps of silver were to be seen.

"You know," Tonto offered as they rotated to trek back and search the next fissure. "Maybe they abandoned this place because it actually is worthless now. Perhaps they excavated all the silver and elected to leave the mines in idleness."

"Yeah, maybe." She whacked a rock aside with a boot. "But haven't you seen the tools lying around, the picks and the other lanterns? They were planning on coming back. So why didn't they?"

"Perchance Vukodlak frightened them away." He chortled and shook his head. Kim stiffened.

"Maybe so." She murmured, a hand flying absently to her scar, tracing the slightly raised route to her jawline.

"Scout?" Tonto exclaimed, surprised to find his mount outside the crater, head bowing up and down as if in greeting. "Where's Heaven-Bound?" He pondered, probing with his eyes for the other horse.

"Where else?" Kim shrugged, pressing her lips into a thin line. "Running home, in town, anywhere so long as it's at a distance from me. That horse has a loathing for me, almost worse than the abhorrence I have for myself." She snorted and dragged a hand through her tousled hair.

"Stupid animal," Tonto said, placing hands on his hips. "It doesn't know who it carries."

"No, he understood precisely who he bore." She glanced along the lip of the quarry and her spine tingled, her face beginning to twitch. "In any event, I'm thinking he was more clever than we are. Can you hear it?" She asked, turning a complete circle to obtain a better view of the pit's edge.

"Yes." He whispered after a moment, swallowing tightly. "Where are all the night creatures?"

"Humans weren't the only things that deserted this place, it seems all of life has." A chilly gust whistled through the gorge and came careening into the lantern's flame, nearly extinguishing it. To Kim, it felt as if the entire realm of darkness was bearing down on her in that instant and the only light in the whole world was the one she held; the tiny pin-prick of softly glowing fire in the harsh night.

"Kimberly." Tonto hissed softly from behind her. Kim's head jerked his way; no one dared call her that, not after the accident.

He subtly motioned upward, towards the quarry's border, his gaze never wavering from the place. Kim spun slowly, uneasy of what she'd see. The lamp's tarnished handle almost slipped from her faltering grip. Her eyebrows leapt beneath the black mask and her brow furrowed in disquiet.

Overhead a single creature crouched, waiting. Steadily its companions materialized from the evening haze, encircling the mine. Dozens of the beasts peeled away from the darkness, each snarling down at them, bearing long fangs that gleamed yellow in the moonlight. Their eyes cast dark red shadows, hatred emanating from within. For the first time, Kim got a clear view of the beings who'd introduced so much disorder to her life: their bodies were enormous, double the size of even the largest canine and twice as muscular as the strongest of animals. Their pelts, course and ragged, jutted out in abnormal positions and rippled in odd patterns along their sturdy limbs. Saliva dripped in steady rivulets from their gigantic mouths, dribbling over extended tongues and pointed teeth.

For several seconds, which felt like an eternity, the monsters remained, growling deeply from their throats. Seething, some began to pace back and forth. Others lingered motionless, glowering. "They won't come into the quarry." Kim whispered, stating this for her partner's peace of mind.

Tonto broke his stare from the scene that had mesmerized him, turning halfway toward his companion. "Pardon?"

"They're not going to chance it down here. Silver, remember?" She said, hefting the light in a more solid grip.

"Right," Tonto pulled in a breath and hoped that was true. If Kim was nervous at all, she hid it well. "How do we get back?"

"Suppose we'll have to wait them out, spend the night here." She replied, patting the white stallion and then Scout in reassurance.

"In the open like this?" Tonto inquired, anxiety tightening his voice.

"I figure we'll make camp in one of the caves, concealed from certain eyes." Kim said, glancing upward quickly. "Surely there must be a cavern large enough for the horses to hide in also." Tonto nodded, uneasiness still playing its fearful tune over him.

As they passed beneath the creatures on the ledge, each would offer a pitted howl or high-pitched whine; several leapt up on their hind legs and lurched about, yearning to come near but not finding the courage.

Kim's cheek crawled and throbbed, her scar pulsated as if someone had kindled a fire at its base and her face was steadily burning. She was confident that if they didn't find someplace out of the way soon she would collapse.

Tonto led Scout under an overhanging archway, Kim trailing him with the white stallion on her heels. "This ought to do." Tonto supposed, sliding the rope halter over his mare's chocolate ears. "It's an improvement from out-of-doors, at least. Perhaps we can go deeper in," He peered into the rock-strewn expanse. "We could search for a place to light a meager blaze."

Kim was silent and compliant, her stomach twisting horribly. Outside their hollow all had once again grown tranquil; her flesh no longer heaved, though the sensation lingered faintly. Had the beasts departed? If that was so, what had beckoned them away? She was their chief target after all, was she not?

Chapter 10

The fire's glow flickered off the back wall of the cave, surrounding them in a warm blanket of light. Kim sat huddled in a corner. Her ridged back pressed against the rock, she stared with steady eyes into the flashing tongues of the blaze – vast mystery was confined within the erratic dancing of the flames. She exhaled deeply and repositioned her cramping legs. Looking up, she caught sight of Tonto who sat cross-legged just opposite of her. He appeared quite absorbed in his inspection of a bedroll for mildew.

Tonto had stumbled upon a far grander cavern in his quest for burnable materials. Farther in, he'd discovered crevices stocked with old blankets and rags, water canteens, and ancient tin cans. He'd loaded an ample amount into his arms, nearly suffocating from the odor of decay that clung to the belongings, and relocated the supplies to their own cave. He had apologized for the absence of anything nutritional and she'd shrugged. Tonto was a strange mystery in and of himself. Where, really, had he come from? Why had he chosen to endure these circumstances with her? What was to gain?

"Tonto," she whispered softly. He glanced up briefly from his assessment of the bedding and elevated an eyebrow as if to ask *what?*. "Where'd you learn to speak English the way you do?"

He licked his dry lips, dark eyes returning to the task in his hands. "My mother taught me, and my father, the Indian's tongue. I was raised in both worlds, the sophisticated and the untouched." He peered up passed the smoking fire, staring at the far wall, his hands moving mechanically through the cloth in his lap. "You see my mother wasn't an Indian, she was one of the first English settlers who, after numerous years, ventured into Ranger's Valley. My father, a warrior of the tribe, took her as his wife. She bore him a son, christening the youth Tonto.

"From the earliest times she taught me things no other Indian knew or has known. In certain moments I have recalled several of her instructions, and at other whiles all she is to my mind is a shadow and feelings. Joyful, she was continuously full of contentment and peace. She appreciated her life, even amongst those who were not her ancestral kin. She showed me how to speak, to write, and read. She imparted unto me the understanding of a God who covers sin. Most of these lessons I can yet remember, but countless are blurred and missing.

"One day my mother set out to gather the lately ripened blackberries. She never returned with life in her. They said a mountain lion attacked her. My father didn't believe that. He vowed vengeance on her killer and took it upon himself to catch the so-called animal and slay it. His body was later discovered deep in the forest thickets, undistinguishable but for the golden band on his finger, a gift from my mother. They were both buried in the glade, beneath the very cross you clung to on the evening you lost your own family." The blanket twisted in his hands, his mindless task forgotten. He tossed the cloth aside, gazing across the expanse between them. "Now you tell me something. What transpired that night?"

Kim's brow knit and she bit her lip. "Anything I would gladly give you knowledge of, but not that," she mumbled, scowling down at her worn boots so as not to meet his stare.

"You might be surprised," Tonto replied, stirring the coals absently with a pickaxe's wooden grip. "Speaking of matters often benefits the one who's been holding an event too tightly in their mind."

"For some that may bring relief, however I'm different." Kim clarified. But was the actual reason for her resistance an unwillingness to confess to her closest comrade that she had been the cause of her family's passing? That she had been the selfish sour child? "You wouldn't want to know me before this."

"Well, the you right now is rather unfeeling in and of itself. What could be worse?" Tonto sent a wink in her direction, indicating he'd meant it as a jest.

"Right." She rolled her dark eyes, gradually snaking her fingers up to remove the sheath of coarse fabric from about her face. Tonto's penetrating stare lingered on her and she squirmed uncomfortably. After a minute of unpleasant silence had strained by, she spoke. "You truly wish to understand?" Kim perceived him to be nodding, though she did not turn to look. Swallowing stiffly, she yielded. "I'll tell you what happened."

Kim drew herself up onto her knees, outlining a squiggly path in the thin layer of loose dirt that covered the hard-packed soil beneath her. "Father wanted to leave; Ranger's Valley had long lost its hold on his heart. Everything he did was a game. He wore the guise of a considerate caretaker but in his mind he loathed the settlement and its inhabitance. Mother detested it as well. She used to continually state that a sandy, uncultured dustbowl was no place to raise children. They would exchange views about departing late at night when they assumed no one else could hear.

"One day my parents informed me I had been engaged to be married. My father had arranged it. No say of mine was sought for, the betrothal simply stood. This was the excuse they had been waiting for as the lad I was to wed lived to the north in the city. They packed our belongings and that very eve, when twilight descended, we mounted a carriage that would transport us to our new home. I watched my childhood fade away; I never got to say goodbye to it, or to anyone." A small pebble became the stagecoach on her dirt-line road and she pressed it onward.

"I can remember the moon's pale face and the murky shadows in the timbers as we travelled through. I recall wishing my existence was changed. I can still see them in my mind's eye. They haunt my dreams; the silhouettes of their bodies hurtling through the lofty trees behind us, alongside us, all around us. I saw them. I didn't recognize them for what they were but I ought to have said something." She struck the stone down hard halfway over the squiggly mark.

"They attacked us. Killed our driver and horses then dragged the others out of the carriage and were coming in after me." Kim squeezed her eyelids shut, picturing the scene in her mind. "I did the only thing I could think of: I ran. Faster and further then I'd ever run before, and I didn't look back. I stumbled upon the clearing and there I collapsed. I felt as if death had already claimed me and knew too soon that would be a reality. I clung to your mother's cross and wept into the darkness, but it was for me that I sobbed. For *my* loss, *my* pain, *my* passing presently to be, *my* wish that was granted; it was all about me." She shook her head, splaying a hand flat across the make-shift road and pebble.

"The creatures had tracked me but for some peculiar reason they wouldn't cross into the glade. Something held them back. I don't recollect much after that, but one of them clawed open my face." Her clenched fingers flitted to her jaw. "And that's all I remember." Kim fell silent, but inside her the emotions stirred. Her heart thumped faster. Where was the numbness? She needed it to keep her safe from unwelcome sentiments, to hide herself in and to get lost in indifference. Steadily the coldness returned, the abnormal sensation fleeing before the surge of her emotionlessness.

"Life is a battle. One enemy may be overcome, but there will always be another." Tonto sighed and continued speaking. What he said seemed true and Kim was certain he had her own benefit in sight, but she tuned him out. She couldn't afford to feel like that again.

Tonto shifted his position, rolling onto his side and smacking the rock protrusion with his forehead. He lurched away, pressing both hands over his face. "Uhhg." He groaned, slowly turning to lay limply on his back. Vacantly he blinked up at the ceiling and massaged his temples.

"Rise and shine, buttercup." Kim said sarcastically. She stood silhouetted by the cavern's entrance, the coals of the late-night fire buried beneath the soil and the horses frolicking eagerly outside. "I found our silver mine."

Tonto hurriedly sat up, brushing clingy sand from his shoulders. "Really?" He beamed and cracked his neck to one side. "Oh," He grimaced. "I'm so sore."

"Uh huh." Kim grunted, sounding completely unimpressed.

He rose stiffly to his feet, dusting off his clothing as he stood. "I take it the creatures departed then."

Kim's eyes narrowed. Had he truly neglected to notice their absence in the night? She deliberately bypassed responding to his remark. "Come on, we have a lot yet to get done and a long path to travel homeward. I'd rather not get stranded in the desert at dusk."

"But," Tonto raised a finger into the air for emphasis. "We'll have silver."

Kim rolled her eyes, traipsing out through the cave into the main quarry and the broad, bright sunlight. "The gigantic fissure you discovered last evening is grander than you initially imagined. They delved quite deeply into the mine's wall, it goes on for some time and ends abruptly in a giant, flat stone panorama. It almost appears as if someone took paint and glazed the entire thing in silver." She shrugged. "I don't know if there's just a thin coating of it or if it actually goes deeper. In either instance, I can see why they would have chosen that cave to store their provisions."

"It would be the logical choice." Tonto agreed, patting Scout on the rump as they wandered past. "In any case, we have plenty to complete today." He gazed absently at the cloudless sky, musing to himself. "I wonder if Will's found out anything new."

Kim scowled at the mention of the young chaplain's name. "That doesn't really concern us. He's there, we're here. Try to focus."

"I'll do my best," Tonto declared stoutly. "But on particular days I'm simply all over the place. I blame you for that."

Kim huffed. "And why, may I ask, do you find me responsible?" Her words were clipped with annoyance.

"My, we're irritable at present aren't we?" Tonto shook his head and sent a pebble ricocheting into the quarry's open spaces with the heft of a boot. "I was merely observing how you cause me to jump around in an effort to keep up. You have bad mood swings."

"And I blame you for that." She snorted. "Come along, time's wasting."

The white stallion hadn't left them. Even after they'd uncovered the miners trail out of the quarry area he'd shadowed Kim's footsteps wherever she went. They had finally given up shoeing him off and trusted that once they departed for town he'd meander his way home.

Tonto hoisted himself up onto Scout's back, situating his seat further forward than normal so Kim could climb up behind him. As she positioned herself and prepared to mount, the glossy steed nudged her arm with his soft, grey nose and nickered. He heaved his head to one side and knelt down with his forelegs on the ground. Kim swallowed her surprise; did he mean for her to ride him?

"This could prove entertaining." Tonto smirked, clicking Scout into a half turn so he could observe. "Don't fall off when he gets up."

Kim directed a hooded glare his way and swung her leg lightly over the stallion's hunched back, steadily leaning her entire weight into the horse. The animal tossed his mane from his black eyes and thrust his feet under him, flicking his tail as he rose. Kim sat rigidly straight. The two passed a breathless Tonto as if they had been riding together their whole lives. "Shut your mouth before you attract flies." Kim advised her companion once she'd trotted out several feet in front of him.

Tonto nudged Scout into a jog, coming up alongside them with a wide grin spread across his tanned face. "Looks to me as if you got yourself a new partner. He's made it fairly clear he's going with you."

Kim allowed a gaunt smile to pass over her lips. "Appears so."

"A name," Tonto explained. "You'll need to assign him a title now. A noble steed deserves a stout name. You can't call him *horse* forever."

Kim nodded, running a hand along the snowy stallion's neck. "Silver," She whispered. "The fright of the Asgaya-wahya and the steadfast friend to the hunter. Silver."

The town seemed darker than usual. The lanterns had been lit and suspended from nails illuminating the doorways of certain shops. From the saloon ruckus echoes emerged, but from the chapel's sanctuary only silence rose to meet their ears. Even the modest lamp dangling by a pole over the entry had no life in it. Perhaps William hadn't been expecting them, and why would he? They hadn't informed him when they expected to return. Kim felt slight relief. She really hadn't wanted to pay a visit but Tonto had insisted on it and she'd finally consented.

Halting their mounts near the porch, they delayed in silence for a long moment, staring up at the shadow-cloaked church house. "Do we just…go in?" Kim wondered.

Tonto shrugged and slid to the ground. "I'll take a peek, see if he's asleep." He disappeared into the building on noiseless feet.

Kim slipped off of Silver's bare-back; stroking his neck she worked her fingers through his shiny coat. He bowed his head to peer at her and snorted, throwing his mane. "Where did you even come from?" She whispered into his face, gazing intently at his swimming black eyes. "What adventures have you already seen?"

"He's not here." Tonto's voice carried from the doorway. He took the outer steps swiftly, landing in the soft dirt of the roadway.

"Not inside?" Kim's brow furrowed, her stomach twisting. "Are you positive?" She peaked over her stallion's ears, toward the gloomy entrance.

Tonto dipped his chin in assurance. "The entire place is vacant, there is no William within. I am confident." He stated, words steady.

"Mayhap he's calling on individuals at the saloon, probing for information." She offered with a forged disregard.

Tonto seized Scout's harness, striding up equal with Silver. "That's viable. If naught else someone may know where he can be found."

'Surely,' Kim supposed. Picking up her boots, she paced behind Tonto, crossing the bare street, her horse trailing along without being prompted. *'Or he might have been ushered away to the city. Perhaps father Maximus desired his company.'* Coupled with this casual thought were the memories, reminders of the last undertaking to travel the lengthy route to the north.

"Kim," She snapped her eyes forward, at the voice, heaving her recollections aside. "Are you coming?" Tonto inquired. He stood with a hand gripping one of the double-hinged doors, the calm, glowing light from inside silhouetting his dark features.

"Yes," she replied distractedly, mounting the weathered wooden steps.

Tonto narrowed his gaze and gave her a hard stare. Whirling unexpectedly, he pushed his way into the cheerful surface room of the tavern. A complete hush washed over the place like a rushing flood and every head turned in their direction – an Indian and the masked stranger.

Kim could read the questions, concern, instant dislike, and utter curiosity displayed visibly on each face. Some wore mixtures of emotions while others had their features set hard to one extreme or another. But they were all of them shocked. Kim fixed her jaw, taking a step forward. Her black rawhide boots clunked on the timber-slatted floor, her right hand tucked half into her belt. Tonto strode in step with her, his eyes riveted straight ahead.

The bartender swallowed nervously, his Adams apple bouncing. "What can I do ya fer?" He asked, spinning a mug over a loose cloth in his palm.

"Drinks." Kim said, lowering her vocal range. "The less strong ones."

The majority of the inhabitance turned back to their games, conversation and gossip, though each had a sense trained on the two foreigners.

Kim settled herself on a bar stool and leaned forward on her elbows. Tonto remained standing, pressing close to her left shoulder, arms crisscrossed over his wide chest. "We're looking for chaplain William. Have you seen him?" He inquired of the man who was conveying the diminutive glasses full of neutral colored liquid toward them.

The bartender wiped his sweaty hands on the discolored apron hooked around his middle and regarded each of their expressions; both equally frozen. "Aye, I seen 'im. He came'n 'ere lookin' fer somethin'. Don't know if 'n he ev'ry found it, though I do recall that big 'ol feller, Glibson, Gillon?," He scratched his balding scalp. "Was riled up somethin' awfil by 'im. The two of 'em disappeared a might ago. Don't know where ta, or if'n they were together or not." He shrugged, hopeful the report appealed to their fancy.

Kim's heart beat faster; her mind churned and she glanced sideways at Tonto. The giant man? The very same they had come across in the past few days? The man who didn't seem to greatly appreciate them? What could he want with William, a minister?

Tonto freed his upper limbs, setting a few coins on the table. Neither of them had touched their draughts. He touched Kim gently on the shoulder, triggering her to rise. The two strolled out of the saloon without saying another word.

Gawking eyes surveyed them, and countless sighed in relief at their passing. They straddled their horses and galloped north, both of their thoughts rationalizing relatively the same thing; the enormous, unfavorable man was most definitely not whom he pretended to be.

Chapter 11

Kim draped herself in the quiet of her own remote world, the shadow-laden timbers flashing by in her peripheral vision. They jogged swiftly through the dim woodland, their course fixed for home. Silver's gait was smooth beneath her and she could make out the gusts of his steamy exhalation in the forest's chill air. Kim endeavored to take a deep breath but the biting breeze constricted her throat with frigid fingers. Contemplations and opinions invaded her effort at an empty mind and she battled internally with the horrors her consciousness conceived.

Suddenly, Tonto seemed very far ahead, his form distancing into a vague shape. Silver had begun to slow his rapid pace and slackened unexpectedly into a measured walk. His ears flicked, perking forward to listen. Presently she lost sight of her comrade in the overhanging mist before her, but Kim did not urge Silver into a faster stride. She rode on in silence, alone.

Silver halted, motionless, his hooves planted and his legs tense. Kim could feel the apprehensive power building in his muscles; if anything spooked him, he'd be off like a shot and she would doubtless end up sitting on the rutted path. The stallion snorted softly. Lowering his neck, he dropped easily to his knees, allowing her to scramble off. Kim slithered over his snowy back in dumbfounded compliance. What was he doing? Why was she dismounting? And had Tonto truly not noticed her absence?

She stepped backward, distancing herself from Silver and was preparing to open her mouth when he sprung away. In a white blur he veered off the trail and pounded deeper into the timberland. Kim's eyes widened and astonishment tingled in her stomach mixed with the searing sting of betrayal. She'd dared to believe this steed would endure as a companion for her, but the horse had abandoned her, just like everyone else – Heaven-Bound, Tonto, the entire cosmos. Kim felt a cry welling up in her throat; she clenched her fists and swallowed bitterly.

A resonating scream rose into the air just beyond the nearest trees, an icy, bodiless wail of vengeance. Her blood ran cold and an unfamiliar sensation coursed over her flesh. Anger was no longer in her mind for fear had broken loose and was surging inside. Kim backed herself to a nearby oak. Hands trembling, she hunkered down at the base between two bent roots. Her voice wouldn't have been able to stem forth if she'd wanted it to and her eyes darted about in frenzied panic – Kim realized she had lost control over her own body to this new emotion.

Another grisly howl erupted behind her hiding place. Kim started at the unearthly bellow, pressing her torso father into the tree's rough bark. A horse's distressed whinny filled the space between the angered cries, and the pounding of hooves could be heard and felt through the leaf-strewn soil. A white streak flickered into sight across the way, deep in the twisting wood, and hounding it was at least ten of the hulking creatures. Each of them bayed after their prize, snapping and snarling at one another as they ran. Kim's heart soared into her throat. Would they realize she was there?

In but an instant they were out of her sight and Kim's pent up breath was released. She sagged against the oak, hoping upon hope they wouldn't overtake Silver.

A warm, gusty waft blustered over her, a rank stench assaulting her nostrils. Kim's eyes began to water and her stomach turned dangerously. She seized the tree root on her right, clenching it with whitening knuckles and dared not to blink; something was on the opposite side of her wooden refuge.

Ever so slowly, Kim twisted her head to peek around the lumpy bark and there, not three feet away, stood the foulest animal she'd ever beheld. Dark and hairy, torn and scabbed, bleeding and salivating, the beast gazed off into the thickets beyond. What did it notice? Why hadn't it smelled her yet? Kim's mouth went dry. The creature would discover her soon enough. She pushed her back and shoulders hard into the tree. Closing her eyes, she waited for the inevitable.

What seemed like an eternity passed until finally Kim cautiously peeled open her eyes, peeping once again around the oak. The monster lingered in the same position as it had when she'd first perceived it: staring into the murky woodlands. It sneezed, muzzle dipping towards the ground. Kim jumped and clapped a hand over her mouth to muffle her yelp of surprise. The animal snorted and threw its massive head, moseying a few more feet away from her sanctuary. Unexpectedly, it caught the echoes of a far off clamor and dove into a sprint, dashing onto the rugged roadway that wove through the forest. A shaft of bright moonlight dripped down through the upper foliage, illuminating the creatures undulating form. Tearing through the timbers was no longer a four-legged animal, but a man of lofty stature and dim shadows. Kim leaned forward in disbelief, her safety all but forgotten as she tracked his course into the night. He didn't look familiar with his tar black hair, rough clothing, innumerable scars that cut up and down his dense arms, and thick crimson liquid oozing in peculiar patterns from several of the wounds.

Kim gagged at the overpowering odor he'd left lingering by her hiding spot. She retracted into the oak once more. So that was how the followers of Vukodlak walked amid the armies of the kingdom brother and instigated chaos. They could effortlessly change their figure as it pleased them. She shuddered inside herself.

Kim's heart thumped faster in her chest and she gasped at the feelings that were overwhelming her. The numbness was a fading pleasure. At the moment floods of emotions were washing in with no reserve. She staggered to her feet and sprinted into the thicket in the direction of the village. Her awareness churned like a disturbed puddle after a summer rain and her vision wouldn't focus on anything. The earth beneath her boots appeared to be heaving, and her feet tangled and slipped. She plummeted to the dirt, crying into the ground. The barrier that protected her had shattered inside and everything all at once seemed to be falling on her, striving to break her in half. She writhed in the cold soil, crawling her way over to a scrawny, half-fallen sapling. And there she sat, hands covering her head and her head on both knees. She gulped for air.

A stick snapped nearby and she bit her lip, her body quivering. Glancing over her shoulder and the upper portion of the tree, she saw three of the creatures assembled together snarling and spitting at one another. Kim squeezed her eyes shut, horrors and nightmares she'd either forgotten she had or never knew about came gushing onto her mind's eye. The compelling urge to scream piggybacked the images. But, as much as her thoughts and heart yearned to cry out, she held it in.

Throwing another look at the beasts, she saw, this time, that they stood in human form, giant and looming. They seemed to be conversing but she could perceive no words. Abruptly they spun and loped off, a firm purpose in their bloody eyes. They sprinted into the darker shadows of the trees, and as they leapt a transformation came over their bodies so that when their feet collided with the ground it was on four paws.

Kim sealed her eyes tightly, tiny tears seeping passed her lids. Her erratic breathing began to steadily slow as the minutes trickled by and she inhaled strongly the evening air. A cold and clammy appendage slithered over her mouth and clamped hard against her sweaty skin, causing her already burning scar to blaze furiously. Kim shrieked through the flesh wrapped over her face and her body instinctively fought back.

"Kim!" Tonto hissed, jerking his hand away and leaping out of her kicking range.

Kim ceased her flailing instantly and stared up at him, hurt choking her features.

He stood a horse-length away, massaging his thigh. "You must be more cautious who you lash out at! You could pulverize someone."

She rose, wiping at her nose with a single gloved hand, the other reaching out toward him. Tonto sidled away, both palms facing her. "I understand you didn't intend to harm me. I'm alright. Just be careful next time."

She nodded in agreement and swallowed, observing his face searchingly. Finally, sure of her own voice, she spoke. "Did-did you see that?"

He looked up earnestly and met her anxious gaze. "Yes. It is not something I wish to witness again." He examined the woodland about them and, taking her by the arm, stealthily maneuvered them closer to the path they would take homeward.

He whistled for Scout. "Where is Silver?" He inquired.

Kim's chin sank. "I don't know. He let me down then took to the bramble thickets in the deep woods. At first I believed he'd abandoned me, but I think," She swallowed, forcing the terror that still stormed inside to slacken. "I think he was leading the creatures on, keeping them from noticing my presence. I heard awful noises..." She trailed off into silence.

"I'm confident he's alive. He seemed exceedingly clever." Tonto reassured. "We must get on to the village. Nevertheless, I'm positive he'll show up before this all comes to an end."

Kim bowed her head, her mind once again discovering the numb place she ached to hold onto – the mental state where feelings were void and nothing mattered.

Scout trotted into view amid the mossy-barked trees. Slowing to meet them, she shook her long face, throwing her lengthy, brown mane about. The saddle bags, packed to bursting with silver flecks, bounced at her flanks. At least Tonto's mare would be untouchable for the beasts; they should have evenly distributed the parcels.

Tonto mounted and stretched an arm down for Kim who scrambled up behind him. Her face pulsated faintly and she sensed the eyes of numerous creatures boring into her. They wouldn't assault her at the present, but they wouldn't let her alone forever. Someday she would be trapped without defense; someday she'd have a choice to make.

The following morning Kim stirred to the sound of her adopted brother excitedly jabbering in his own language. He knelt beside her bedroll and shook her by the shoulders, bouncing back to his feet the next instant. "What?" She murmured, sleep thickening her voice.

Kim shoved the heavy pelt off her torso and over her knees. She slipped her raw-hide boots over her breeches and groggily allowed the enthusiastic five-year-old to lead her from the enclosed tent. Flipping the tanned flap, Kim took a single step and then stood still, her feet planted and her hands dangling loosely at her sides. The breeze tossed her long, auburn hair, flipping it lightly about her neck and face. She dragged nimble fingers through the lengthy strands and drew it back.

Silver stood erect and ridged in the midst of the village as if he'd been hewn out of white stone, not even the wind seemed to stir his mane. The Indians flocked about him like clucking hens, but he simply remained as he was, slowly looking her way. He snorted and bobbed his head vigorously, parting the throng of people to stride toward her. Kim fixed a hand on her hip and couldn't help but smile a little. He'd not been torn to pieces. That was good.

The stallion ambled over and peered down his nose at her. She raised an eyebrow. He gradually bowed his head in submission and Kim smirked, rubbing his ears. "Thank you." She whispered. He snorted, shoving her with his forehead; she sidestepped quickly to maintain her balance. "Don't be stupid." She chided, rolling her eyes, though truthfully her heart was delighted to see him.

Tonto trotted by, Scout already beneath him. He grinned and motioned with a hand for her to join them; there was much to do on this day. Kim nodded. Ducking swiftly into her shelter, she snatched the hat and mask beside her bedroll from the pelt floor. Throwing the tanned fabric over her hair, she tucked the cloth disguise into her belt as she exited. Kim swung up onto Silver's back before he could kneel for her, preferring the people of the village didn't know everything.

Presently, she caught up with Tonto, their mounts striding neck in neck. They reduced their speed to enjoy the smoother gait and to exchange thoughts.

"We need to secure the talents of someone who can shape the silver. We should probably attempt to learn where William disappeared to, what, if anything, he found out, and I need to find an alternative to wearing hats." She scowled up at her second creased black one and swiped it off. Reaching her fingers back, she secured the makeshift mask about her face and replaced the wrinkled hat.

"The last one sounds rather urgent." Tonto let his smile fade as the moment of humor slipped by.

"What kind of weapon were you thinking of molding the metal into?" He inquired.

"I don't know for certain. I believe trying to produce a larger knife from the lesser flecks would be nearly impossible. So I was thinking something lighter and more manageable; an object that can be created in mass so we won't ever be without it. Some article that we can carry on our persons. I'm not sure exactly what it will be yet."

"I suppose it would also be to our advantage if the smith could produce these objects fairly quickly. Perhaps I can inquire as to what would be best suited for us, as I've acquainted myself with the smith once before. You ought to search for a letter or something of the like that William may have left behind to say where he was going. I'm positive he wouldn't just up and leave without notice. He seemed too cautious for that."

"Cautious?" Kim snorted. "He wasn't very cautious when he told us everything he knew, or when he offered to look for information. Maybe it was his carelessness that called him away from the settlement." She ranted, gripping a bit of Silver's snowy mane in her fist.

Tonto shook his head in disagreement. "I doubt that very much. He was simply a genuinely friendly individual. You can't hold that against him merely because you're not."

Kim's lips tightened into a straight line and she glared ahead. At times Tonto cut right to the point and even if he was correct she hated it. Was she actually that nasty, that irritable? Kim sighed and dropped her gaze, ashamed she had the temperament she did. Back in the old days it had been most difficult to anger her; she'd been earnestly content and jubilant. Why had everything changed so much? What had she possessed back then?

Kim's numbness fluttered inside. Her hands flexed and she clamped her teeth together. Perhaps she had once been able to feel, but that was not something she was willing to let happen again. Pain accompanied emotions and what good was suffering?

Chapter 12

Kim's dark gloves ruffled over the scattered papers on the desk, her eyes skimming the area for anything that resembled a note or letter. Her fingers leafed through the individual sheets but there was nothing significant among them. She huffed out a breath, crossing her arms to gaze about the overcrowded room. The chamber was quite chaotic, yet everything had its precise place. She slapped her palms onto her hips and glared about, confused and uncertain where to start next.

Books and volumes still lay spread about the entire apartment, though if possible more appeared to be on the floor. The one Will had been flipping through the afternoon before last had been propped open and left on the low-sitting table. Kim gently stole it from its resting spot and scanned the yellow-edged pages, the scent of an ancient tome drifting to her nose. She closed her eyes for a moment, savoring the scent; she'd always liked that smell. A thin slip of off-white paper slipped out as she turned a page and twirled in a zigzag route to land on her boot. Kim bent at the waist and caught the sheet up. Several minutes passed before her mind completely registered what it said. The book slid from her grasp, plunged to the pile of other manuscripts by her feet, where it settled – splayed half-open.

"What would be the lightest to transport? The most easily accessible?" Tonto queried. After getting over the initial shock of the Indian's ability to speak perfect English, the farrier had been a bit more obliging.

The black smith chucked a finished shoe into the water bucket and scratched his stubbly chin. He glanced up at the native, uncertain as to what the boy was looking for exactly. "I don't rightly know," He mused for a moment, staring out into the clouded sky. "Knives is pretty light, like ya said. Not always easy ta carry a lot of 'em though." He took a long thought-out breath, pinching his features together. Running a filthy hand through his wavy hair, Jeb pursed his lips. "Bullets a're easier to make bunches of quick like. They're not too hefty of ya shape 'em right, and they can be stowed easy enough in a gun belt." He shrugged. "Just 'nother option. What da ya need 'em fer anyhow? That'd make t'all the difference." He speculated, casting suspicious eyes on the dark-skinned lad.

"Tonto!" Kim exclaimed from across the street. She leaped down the chapel's outer steps and mounted Silver in a heartbeat, urgency driving her actions.

Tonto dipped his chin in gratitude to the black smith. "I'll be back with a better idea of what I'd like." He sprinted to Scout's side and, gathering up the reins in his hands, clambered onto her back. Kim had already prodded Silver into a canter and was flying out of the settlement as if one of the creatures was pursuing her. He wheeled Scout away from the barn and clicked her into a jog and then a gallop.

Tonto caught up with her just past the farthest post which marked the end of the arid road leading into town. He maneuvered Scout ahead of the other horse and pulled up suddenly, forcing Silver to halt swiftly so they wouldn't collide. Kim's face was set but her hands jittered by her sides.

"What's wrong?" Tonto probed gently, concerned. Scout shuffled her feet, stomping at the flies. "Why'd you take off so abruptly?"

Kim's expression went slack, and she blew through pursed lips. "I needed to talk to you, away from everyone else. This was the fastest and most hassle-free way I could think of at the time."

"Not very subtle." He muttered, hands splayed over his knees.

She snorted, withdrawing a slim piece of ripped paper from her belt. Without a word, she offered it to him. Sitting back with arms crossed at the wrists, Kim waited for his response.

Tonto examined the page, his eyebrows rising then falling. "So," He began, passing her back the slip. "What's all this supposed to mean?"

"Don't you understand?" She tested quietly.

"Aside from it being printed rather sloppily – I'd assume in haste – and besides the fact that Will's name is signed below, I'm not entirely positive we're thinking the same thing. You appear to comprehend his words perfectly; perhaps you'd care to share your thoughts."

"It's not specifically clear, to be certain, but who else, Tonto, then that hostile man we encountered at the inn? The same one who likewise took us to see William in the first place." Kim exclaimed avidly. "He's one of them, an Asgaya-wahya. A follower of Vukodlak."

"The giant irritable fellow." Tonto said, testing the sound of it on his tongue.

She nodded strongly. "I had this sense when we first encountered him, something inside me burned and my face..." She absently traced her scar towards her jawline. "I didn't like him, and he certainly didn't appreciate us. I doubt he enjoys Will's company either, that's why something happened the night we were trapped in the quarry." Her brow furrowed. "Remember that evening? After we'd gone into the cave, almost before, the creatures disappeared. Something, or someone, must have beckoned them away. Maybe that short-tempered man is their leader and he summoned them to..." She glanced into Tonto's face. "To seize William."

Hush descended and thoughts soared with each breath. "But to what end?" Tonto eventually queried, trying not to blatantly state Will could very well be dead.

"I don't know," Kim remarked flatly. "But he's alive." She firmly denounced the opinion he'd failed to say but so visibly had assumed. "I do know where we're going, however." She veered Silver about with her legs, beginning to trek into the taller grass.

"Where?!" Tonto called, prodding Scout into action. "Do I get the high privilege of also knowing this place we're traveling to?"

"North. There's a city in that direction. There is likewise a man who may be able to answer our questions. It's past time we paid him a visit."

"Reverend Maximus," A dark-skinned youth called from the entryway. He stood erect and carried a proper air about him. One of his little hands lingered on the door knob, his finely tailored clothing immaculate. "Someone to see you, sir." He said, keeping his eyes fixed straight ahead.

The timeworn minister chuckled, turning from his place by the window. "I don't think we require all this old formality, James. Please, show the guest in."

"*Visitors,* sir," The boy corrected, persistent in his formal conduct.

"My," The elderly gentleman exclaimed, his deeply wrinkled face beaming, "it has been no trivial amount of time since *two* someone's have come to speak with me. Again I say, please permit them to enter."

"Yes sir." The lad clicked the heels of his finely polished shoes together. Backing out, he gently sealed the door behind him. In a smart march he paraded down to the parlor to retrieve the most peculiar callers he'd ever seen.

Maximus perceived the light rap on the doorframe from his seat by the empty fireplace. "Come in, James," He directed, uncertain why the child chose to continue the civilities.

The colored youth entered soundlessly and dipped his head. "Your visitants, sir." He then stepped to one side, allowing the foreigners passage under the pristine entryway. Snapping his heels once more, he vanished.

Maximus was far too polite to stare, but something about the girl made him study his unexpected visitors more thoroughly. "Welcome!" He rose from the chair out of courtesy, bowing his chin in recognition of their presence. "I'm delighted to offer you the comfort of this chamber and whatever words I can provide you with. Be content to take a seat anywhere. Remove your boots or hat if you feel the need, and take a respite." He waved to several different spots about the apartment where one could sit if they had a liking to.

"Thank you," Kim replied, wandering over to a three-legged stool near the extensive window. She sat hesitantly and hauled the black hat from her windblown hair. Tonto chose to stay on his feet, taking up residence beside her right shoulder.

"I would have requested for tea to be brought up, but I was caught entirely unawares by your arrival," Maximus explained warmly, drawing his own chair closer to his guests. "I am called —"

"Maximus," Kim recited for him, trying to communicate respect through her tone. "We know."

"Oh." He smiled, satisfied they already seemed to be familiar with him. "Then, perhaps, you might spare your own names to an old man, for the sake of this memory of mine? I do not recollect having met you afore."

No one else needed to get hurt, particularly him, her former acquaintance. "This is Tonto." Kim gestured with her opposite arm to her Indian brother. "And most people refer to me as the lone Ranger."

"Ah," The aged minister whispered, his sea-grey eyes twinkling with the secret. "A mysterious title and face." Kim fidgeted under his studying gaze. "How may I assist you?"

"We arrived here from Ranger's Valley," Kim began, impatient to direct the conversation away from herself and on towards the actual purpose of their visit. "You remember that settlement, do you not?"

Maximus nodded, a sad light surging across his countenance. "Aye, I used to have a home and ministry there amongst the fine people. But I grew sick," he paused, peering up from his weathered hands, a profound awareness filling his features. "I've lived here ever since, regaining my strength as the years fly by, but also gaining age. I had hoped to one day return to the town, though now I discern I shan't. I did, however, send a very capable young man in my place, William." He leaned forward eagerly. "Tell me, if you have come from the settlement, you must know of him. How does he fair?"

"It is on William's account that we are here." Kim explained. "He has been seized by the forces of the one called Vukodlak." She observed attentively the ancient man's reaction to her declaration. His eyes resized and he squeezed his hands together firmly. "So you know about this monster." Kim whispered. "You believe he exists."

Maximus spun a distressed face toward her; she'd deceived him into revealing his understanding of the situation. Kim had merely guessed that this brother of darkness had existed but now she knew for certain.

"Yes," The elderly man nodded slowly, sorrowfully. "He is real." Maximus's knuckles faded to white, the debate of his beliefs playing over his worn features. "But I did not think he would come after young William. Will didn't know very much, I made sure of that. I had believed..." His words trailed off into silence.

"It wasn't William who was the threat," Kim protested, swallowing stiffly. "It was me."

The retired chaplain appeared confused, questions running unhindered through his eyes, and for the moment it was as if they were the only two individuals in the entire world. "What?" He breathed.

Kim exhaled sharply. Her life was broken and if she wasn't cautious countless other people's existences would be as well. Nevertheless, Maximus needed to understand what was happening if he was to help them. "I'm the reason Vukodlak snatched William. I'm the cause of the livestock's unnecessary deaths. I'm the motivation for the creatures that slayed Renadear, and I'm also the basis for my family's passing." Hesitantly she reached back and untied the knot at the base of her neck. Removing the mask, Kim let the long, coarse fabric fall away, giving view to her whole face, including the scar. She suppressed her uncertainly, looking up at a past friend, unveiled for the first time in front of one who'd known her prior to the accident.

"Kimberly?" He mouthed. Taking her in, Maximus bit his lip, his bright eyes brimming over with tears. "You were dead," he whispered, pleasure, astonishment, and curiosity layered into his voice. Rising more swiftly then could be thought of a man at his age, the minister enfolded Kim in a tight embrace.

"I am dead," she amended, sucking in a shaky breath.

Maximus distanced himself to arm's length, looking her over with disquiet. "You're changed." He lightly brushed her cheek with a fingertip. "You're marked."

"I've seen his followers. I've encountered them." Kim murmured, shying away from his touch. "However, I didn't come here for a reunion." She reasserted her emotionless state of mind. "I need answers. I need help."

Maximus returned to his seat, sinking deeply into his opinions. "I always taught you the only one who can repair our complications is the great Father, or have you forgotten?"

"I did not forget," Kim retorted, lowering her voice in an attempt to pacify his dismayed thoughts. "But I must be educated on these creatures. I mean to hunt them."

Maximus frowned, his brow puckering, and he shook his greying skull. "That is not wise. They possess dark powers. Wickedness is their mantle and death their shroud. One would not be called prudent to pursue them alone," he clarified.

"But I am not alone," Kim corrected, her facial features set in all seriousness. "My mind is made firm in its cause. With or without your guidance I will be going after William, to the very lair of Vukodlak if need be, and none shall hinder me. I will never rest until he has paid for the deeds of his vile intent."

"Then you shall certainly go to your grave fighting, my dear. Vukodlak is simply one of the numerous forms he can take. The devil is audacious, and his cunning hatred will continue to haunt people long after we are both lifeless in the ground." Maximus persisted in his plea, "Revenge is not yours to dole out. Leave the appointing of righteousness to the One who knows true justice."

Kim rose from the stool, her mask already retied behind her hair, the creased hat in her hands. "I prayed this day would come, when I would once again see the face of one who I knew and they in turn would recognize me. But I had supposed the words would be sweeter, perhaps more considerate." She snorted at her own folly. "I can see you will offer me no sayings of wisdom to fight with and I cannot delay any longer to exchange kinder words. People are dying and it is my doing. I believe I must act, even if you don't think I should or can." She turned abruptly on her heal, stalking towards the white tinted door.

"Wait, child," Maximus called out, halting her march. "I did not say it was wrong to desire to stop these evils that are approaching. But with the improper intentions all is incorrect." He sighed, waving her back. "Sit and I shall convey to you what I know of these vices. Certain things you will be required to learn for yourself, however."

Tonto hadn't shifted a finger throughout the entire conversation and now Kim, too, reclaimed her original position near the glass window. The sun streaked in through the paned glass and danced in odd patterns on the wooden floor.

"You speak of Vukodlak, and yes you'd be correct in that he's an actual being and has been to Ranger's Valley, but you've never set eyes on him for he does not show himself to just anyone. His followers – the Hominem Lupus, the wolf men – are the creatures you've beheld. Like those who are his, Vukodlak can change his figure; and though he can take numerous, altered forms at any time, his faithful are restricted to merely two bodies.

"He is a comrade of the shadows and corruption is his life's blood. It is said he is able to communicate with the Devil himself and was granted his dark magic after performing a task for the dark angel. I cannot tell you much more, other than you will require silver to even wound his creatures. That is everything I am permitting myself to say, except that you Kim must be vigilant. I sense darkness trying to pull itself over you. Do not allow the pain of the past to become the reality of the future."

She stood, reaching out to take his craggy hand. "Thank you. The ache shall not overcome me." She assured, squeezing his worn palm. "I cannot feel."

Maximus watched as the two strangers moved to the door as one and swiftly flowed away as if from a dream. "Be wary, Kimberly. Feeling nothing is almost worse. Be cautious for emotions can break you if you are not prepared for them. And you will feel before the end."

Chapter 13

"I certainly hope whatever it is we're required to learn for ourselves isn't anything that we need to grasp too badly," Tonto reflected spontaneously.

Before the pair had departed for the larger city, they had requested bullets be shaped from the silver they'd collected, trusting the smith would have their order completed by the time they returned. Kim slung the final gun belt around her waist, synching it tight and latching the buckle securely. She stepped off the porch connected to the mercantile and felt the slight heft of her pistols weighing against her thighs. "I hope gunshot was the best strategy," she mused aloud. Catching herself off guard, Kim paused beside the roadway, her mind struggling to replay the first encounter she'd had in the saloon with a filthy rancher. "It's a calling card," she whispered, understanding flooding her consciousness.

"A what?" Tonto asked, his hands wrapped around the revolver on his own belt.

"Somehow he knew. Vukodlak assumed we'd use bullets. He also gambled we'd come looking for him, so he prepared a trail of clues for us to discover." Kim shuffled forward, the heat rising in waves off the dirt road before her.

"Somewhere in that interesting story, Kim, you lost me," Tonto admitted, confused.

She stopped, turning to him with fervor embellishing her words, "When we first came into town and I went probing for information in the saloon, this farmer approached me. He appeared to be a regular customer, but he showed me a silver bullet. Of course I didn't think anything of it at the time, but now..." She rolled her words off into to a pregnant pause. "He also said there were tales he'd heard about a child who'd escaped the accident. 'The lone Ranger to get away with his life.' He went on to comment how the youth died of wounds soon after, but no one could know that unless they'd witnessed the killing personally. He must have been one of them."

"I'm sorry," Tonto interrupted, scratching his head. "I'm not on the same page. How exactly does all this aid us in finding where Vukodlak spends his days?"

"The rancher!" Kim exclaimed, as if the answer were plain as sunlight. "Obviously he's one of Vukodlak's faithful or at least on terms with them. He received the silver bullet and was given stories to tell if someone asked the right questions. Vukodlak wagered we'd figure it out and that I'd remember meeting this man. We simply find this farmer." She looked out at Tonto from under her dark hat. "He can take us to Vukodlak."

"Grange, take a looky here." The slim, stubble-chinned ranch-hand beckoned his companion over. He peered out the crude window, which was truly just a hole in the wall, and pushed his brown hat back further on his head. "Looks ta be company, ta me."

His stout, rather filthy, colleague pried himself out of the partially broken, wooden chair and sauntered over on uneven feet. "Where?" He blinked several times to clear the haze that hung before his unfocused eyes.

"There." A bony finger squiggled out through the glassless frame and jerked towards the rough footpath that led to their collapsing hideaway and surrounding grounds. "See the dust? Whewee, they must'ta be in a dag-on hurry. Wonder what they wan' with us?" His eyes narrowed and he sent a fleeting glance at his counterpart.

Grange sniffed and scratched at the back of his neck. "I don'a like it." He spat onto the dirt floor. "We don' get company less it's bad fer us. Lawmen maybe."

The skinny, weasel-like man hacked. "What'a those kin'a blowhards want with us?" He inquired, lugging out his pistol and inspecting the rounds.

Grange shrugged. "Bet'cha it can't be good." He stumbled sideways over a splintered table in his effort to reach the doorway. "What we gonna do 'bout it?" He slapped white dust off his filthy clothing.

Kramer tossed a second revolver to Grange and motioned around in a circle with his own. "We'll split up, get 'em from both sides 'nd dry gulch 'em."

Grange nodded his consent to the plan, stuffing the gun into his snug belt. "What 'appens if there's more than two?"

Kramer cringed at his partner's proposal. "Oh, hobble your lip. I'll go left, 'round the barn, and you go 'round the horse shed o're there. We'll wait 'til they come a lookin' in here to ambush 'em."

Grange kicked a buckled bench out of his way; Kramer sprang over it and out the door-less entrance, catching his balance as he hastened towards the vacant barn. Glancing back, he beheld Grange wiggling his way through the constricted exit of the house. "Hey!" Kramer shouted, waving his arms above his head. "Get a wiggle on! I'm not getting' lynched fer yer tardiness!"

The heavy man saluted with his hat, heaved through the door, and did a sort of hop-skip around the cockeyed horse shack, concealing himself behind a bulky mound of mildewy straw.

The dust cloud grew and gusted forward, a natural indicator that the riders were drawing ever nearer.

Kramer's fingers constricted over the revolver's trigger, his brow and palms collecting sweat as he waited for the two figures and their horses to appear from the haze. Their forms sharpened though the dust, bowed low over their mounts backs and riding fast. They cantered into the abandoned ranch yard, pulling their horses up in front of the beaten-down farm house and dismounting. A tall, masked foreigner and a dark skinned Indian.

Kramer grunted and watched the lofty one enter the structure, the Indian remaining outside to keep the horses together. Minutes passed and the other's compatriot clambered out from the dilapidated structure to survey the empty area. Hands on her hips, Kramer realized the one in black was a woman; this would be easier than he'd initially assumed. The two were evidently not lawkeepers; perhaps they worked for *him* as well, thus the disguise. Finding out what they sought here would prove interesting, but if they resisted, taking care of them quickly would be the best option.

The female strode over the broken boards that covered the porch and gazed about, her eyes ceasing their rapid sweep at his position. He jerked his head back, unsure if she'd spotted him or not. He'd responded so hastily, Kramer was almost positive she had overlooked him. After a couple minutes seeped past, he stuck his neck out again to reevaluate where his opponents were. The Indian still stood between the white stallion and painted mare, but the tall girl had vanished. Possibly back into the house?

Kramer never perceived the soft tread of boots advancing on him from behind until a gloved hand clasped firmly over his mouth and a cold pistol barrel thrust against his skull. "Make a sound, try to warn your associate, and you may not speak again."

The female hissed close to his ear. Kramer nodded. How did she know he had a partner?

Kim released her strangle-hold on his mouth. Stepping back a few paces, she motioned with her gun for him to drop his weapon to the dirt. "Now," She said slowly, kicking his pistol further off beyond the barn. "Go on out into the open and tell your friend to come out, careful like." He made to protest but she cut him off. "Don't play clever with me; I know there's another chiseler around here, a fat one. Now move."

Kramer gulped and scuttled forward, her steely gaze bearing in on him. Something about her presence was pressing, alarming. Perhaps it was the mask, the black clothing, the four revolvers draped about her waist. Or maybe it was the two thick belts slung across her shoulders and stocked full of shiny bullets that completed her dismaying atmosphere. He couldn't put his finger on it, but her murky cobalt eyes seemed to bore straight though him and he trembled. "Grange?" He hollered, tentatively at first. "Grange, get yer no good, rotten hide out here!" He altered his tone to that of one in charge.

The heavy man shuffled cautiously over from behind the straw pile, his hands poked into the air. He flung the revolver down by Tonto's feet, alarm wrinkling his brow. "What ya want with us?" He inquired as the Indian prodded him towards his counterpart.

Ranger

"You remember me, don't you." Kim pushed Kramer to the side so she could be in full view of the other rancher.

Grange swallowed in fright at the figure before him, but as he looked on his terror began to melt away and a kind of knowing control overcame his attitude. "Aye, I recall ye." He spat into the dirt and reached into his ragged, fraying shirt. He drew out his grubby hand, clutching something in a tightly closed fist. Slowly, Grange extended it toward her, his expression twisting in a wicked grin. The meaty fingers uncoiled and lying in his smattered palm a silver bullet rested, winking up at her. "You came fer this, did'in ya?"

Kim stared at it; her mouth twitching. "No." She stated bluntly, turning away.

Perplexity splashed over the rancher's face, that had been the last response he'd expected. They'd told him someone would come for it. Grange shut his hand, hiding the object from sight, and withdrew his arm. "Then what ye be want'n with us?" He growled. His courage, however slight, had begun to stir.

"What I want?" Kim returned, glancing over her shoulder at the two men. "I want justice."

Tonto urged Scout up beside Silver on the narrow trail so he could exchange thoughts with Kim without the other two questionable characters overhearing. "If Vukodlak sent this rancher into town as bait, aren't we walking into a trap?"

Kim dipped her chin, keeping her eyes locked on the stumbling men in front. "Probably."

"And abducting Will was just extra incentive to get us to charge in there with a head full of steam, right?"

"Most likely."

"And if what Maximus told us regarding this villain is correct, then he has something rather horrible in store for his enemies."

"Oh, undeniably." Kim agreed again, observing their guides tripping through the thorn groves.

"Then why, for the love of everything green and living are we strolling into this like we have no sense!?" Tonto exclaimed, mentally berating himself and lowering his voice. "He's got a thousand followers and five-hundred methods of torture."

"Doubtless more."

"Don't you think it might be sensible to have a strategy of sorts? Or perhaps we should make an effort to sneak in, rather than parading past with guns blazing." Tonto grunted, pushing a tree branch from of his face.

"A plan might be advisable to most. However, even the simplest of strategies can go awry. We have no idea what we're up against. I think perhaps no plan might be more sensible for the time being." Kim decided, her mind churning. She did have a scheme and it was simple. But to share it aloud invited someone to listen in, and thus extra glitches could arise.

Ranger

Tonto was at a loss for words. How could one not have an outline for action? "I don't understand you sometimes, Oginali," He said quietly, his resolve hardening. "But I don't think I can follow you into this fight."

Kim's spine stiffened. So, he would abandon her too, like everyone else. She'd figured his faithfulness was a passing gift and sooner or later this parting would occur. "I'm not asking you to." She swallowed difficultly.

"I know." He reined in Scout's gait. "And I'm not agreeing to." Tonto fell behind, his mare whinnying softly in confusion. "Maybe Maximus was right." He called out, no longer caring who heard his words.

Kim's hand faltered as she patted Silver's neck. She didn't turn her eyes, but his voice carried between them with absolute clarity. "Maybe it was foolish to attempt this scheme. You are alone." Then he was gone, and the woodland seemed dimmer and her errand seemed heavier.

Tonto pressed Scout into a faster sprint, the branches from passing trees lashing at his face and biting into any exposed flesh. Twigs broke beneath the pounding hooves of his horse and brittle leaves were crushed into oblivion. He needed to ride far enough to the west of the main group, so that he could slow and sneak in behind them without being detected. If Vukodlak was ignorant to the fact there were two challengers it would be easier for him to locate William while Kim distracted the Asgayawahya. Tonto's plan was simple; he only hoped Kim had picked up on it. Otherwise, the entire act may have come as a tough blow for her. Her heart, wrapped as it was in layer upon layer of emotional numbness, was still fragile.

Ahead, on his right, Tonto could single out the hum of Grange and Kramer's voices as they murmured together. He quickly slackened Scout's pace and dismounted. Leading her now by the bridle, he slipped carefully around the larger branches and tread lightly over the leaves. If he ventured too close they would surely perceive his footfalls and all would be for naught.

The sunlight had been cut off from the world around them. Now shadows and mist rose from the frosty, hard soil. What little warmth was underneath the surface endeavored to escape in any form imaginable. It was cold, and a deadly chill occupied the stillness. Tonto's heart began to pound more rapidly; a horribly wrong feeling accompanied this place. In all his travels through the forest on hunting expeditions and the like, he'd never entered this portion of the woodlands before. He'd not even seen it from a distance.

The Indian lad perceived Grange's scratchy voice raised a bit louder than afore, as if he addressed Kim without facing her. "We're close. I'd set those guns down and behave if in I weres ya, missy." He chuckled sordidly, the unpleasant sound echoing amid the trees. "The masta' doesn't like people who threaten 'is friends."

Presently, they were marching again and Tonto allowed himself to breathe easier — he'd nearly made it without revealing his whereabouts. He released Scout's harness and signaled for her to halt, hanging the lengthy tether slackly over a tree's mossy branch.

Slowly he crept forward, the stench of decay abruptly overwhelming his senses to the point where he gagged. Tonto wheezed for fresh air but found there was none in the expanse of this forested area. All was stagnant and lifeless. He shielded his nose from the burning sensation and staggered onward. Half bent over, he jogged after the others, afraid of losing them.

Unexpectedly a man appeared in the trail. Towering and foul, he sulked in the gloom a few yards away under the dark vegetation. Tonto dove behind a scraggly tree, a hand clamped over his own mouth. Resting for a moment, he allowed his heart rate to slacken. He was fairly confident the wolf-man hadn't seen him and his assumptions were affirmed when the Asgaya-wahya trekked farther into the timberland. A border scout perhaps?

Tonto took a deep, calming breath, regretted it instantly, and tiptoed out from his hideaway. His dark eyes were sharp, trained to the movement of a single leaf's descent. His ears were keen to the sound of a wing beat. But here, in the murky places of absolute emptiness, there was neither sight nor sound. Here it was simply still. Utter and endlessly nothing surrounded him. Tonto had stolen into the lair of Vukodlak.

Chapter 14

Kim found her hands trembling involuntarily. She seized hold of Silver's mane, gripping it until her knuckles turned white. Her other palm she placed over one of the revolvers on her thigh. The warped trees hunched over them in a kind of crude arc, sheltering the barren pathway. All undergrowth shriveled back from the trail so that nothing but slimy timbers grew as far as one could see.

A vaporous apparition weaved its way towards her. Silver, snorting nervously as the thing drew near, sidestepped to avoid it. The hollow eyes displayed agony and some other passion she did not comprehend. Kim hurriedly looked away. The place was haunted, and all the demons of a thousand souls resided within. This was the den of Vukodlak; this was an abyss of immorality on Earth.

Kim began to feel great regret about her decision to come here unaided. A dark specter loomed inside, threatening to worm its way upward like a plague and quench her courage, but somewhere nearby a friend lurked in the night. She could sense their presence as a soft, pulsing radiance prevailing in the midst of the dense fog. Could it be Will? Or did she have a companion among those of the Asgaya-wahya?

Grange stalked into the approaching darkness with scarcely a fidget, but his colleague, Kramer, looked as if he might have a heart attack.

Kim stroked Silver's neck, reassurance for him as well as herself, and they paced in after the two.

Gradually the trees fanned out into a semicircle around them, creating a miniature, inner glade. Long, dense dark grass swirled about the men and stallion's legs, a quiet breeze drifting ever through it. About the clearing's circumference the wolf-men prowled, more than half their numbers in beast form, the others standing with sneers on their human faces. At the far end of the dell, an elevated, damaged stone throne of roughhewn rock, was situated at a trivial slant. The slate had been blackened with dried blood and charred by numerous fires.

Upon the chair sat a man, if one could call him such, whose beauty was vast and fatal at the same time. His countenance held a youthful air, the wear of the ages having no effect over his appearance. Elongated, black hair dangled passed his shoulders and bright, crimson eyes shot out at her. He seemed to be amused behind the mask of indifference he wore.

The being was not tall but neither was he short, heavily muscled, well-built and not unpleasing in the slightest to behold. Yet something about him set one on edge. His manner looked gracious but shadows flitted at his fingertips and darkness crept up the sides of his cheekbones as if to cloak him from the judgment of one who could see through his disguise.

He rose in one fluent motion, the movement speaking of grace, and an extensive, fluid cape of crimson soared down his back.

"Advance," he spoke, drawing all within earshot to focus on him. The words were commanding yet sweet as a raven's cry.

Grange and Kramer scuttled toward him while Silver hesitated. "All of you," he directed, and Kim urged Silver to take a few more steps.

"Masta'," Grange slurred, prostrating himself low to the ground, fearful to look at him. "I done what ya said, I brought her ta ya like I were supposed ta." He bobbed his head like a bird crooning before its feeder.

"So you did," the handsome leader acknowledged, descending both of the craggy steps from his throne. "You shall be rewarded as is your due." He smiled down at Kramer, the man shrinking into the grass as if he desired to become one with the ground at that moment. "And your associate as well. Asgaya," he called, directing his voice toward the outer circle, and snapped a finger. A pair of men leapt forward, a single creature hounding their footsteps. "Please," He gestured to the ranchers still bowed before him, "take these two to their compensation." Kramer moaned but refused to offer an appeal for mercy as he was dragged away.

Kim had no doubt she would ever see them again among the living. Her eyes tracked the group of men off into the saplings. She had yet to catch a glimpse of William anywhere in this realm.

"Ah, the young Ranger." The man sucked Kim's attention away from her mission, his hands faintly extended. "Welcome. I have long awaited your coming." He smiled, and it appeared as one of warmth and security. "Please, ascend to me," he implored, gesturing at the distance that separated them. To Kim's astonishment the tall grass parted to reveal a stone pathway snaking toward the throne.

"I'd rather stay here," she responded, settling in on Silver's back. Her numbness seemed unaffected by the place even if all other senses were fixed to his command.

He shrugged, accepting her reply and removed himself to his seat. "Welcome to my kingdom. I've been waiting for you." His red eyes narrowed, and a grim smirk eased its way across his unblemished features.

"So you've said," Kim observed bluntly, shifting her posture.

"My, you're a snippy one aren't you?" He chuckled casually. "Always have a comeback, do you?" He steepled his fingers in front of his nose. "But then, I knew you were strong. You'd have to be."

Kim's stomach tumbled; an almost imperceptible change in the pitch of his voice gnawed at her insides. "I'm here for the chaplain; your thugs stole him from me."

"Oh," he cracked his neck to one side, "And here I was, unaware he was *yours*." His features went slack and he sighed dramatically. "Very well."

He waved a hand and the swells of men and beasts divided. The giant man Kim knew only too well stalked down through their ranks, dragging the young minister into the sphere of grass.

William's arms were lashed securely behind his back, his mouth was gagged, and his wavy hair fell into his bright, probing eyes. He appeared to be physically fine, except for a few minor slash-wounds along his forearms and a purple bruise above his left eyebrow that was mostly concealed.

The Asgaya-wahya let him drop onto the turf just inside the tree line, a lengthy distance from her position. If she attempted any sort of risky move, they would kill him before she could react. Kim scowled.

"Now," her rival spoke up, clasping his hands together with an echoing clap, "You can see for yourself Sir William is intact. Speak your mind; there is more to why you're here than simply the liberation of this pathetic man. He alone could not be so dear to you that you would fly into the lair of death itself." His winsome smile flashed. "Tell us," his tone grew quiet and he paused, "of your family."

Kim's impassiveness swelled within her; it wanted out. "I came for you." She declared, her voice steely cold.

"Me?" He asked innocently, his eyebrows lifting. "I'm flattered."

"I know who are, Vukodlak, and I've beheld the things you've done. Do not play games of false

Trista Vaporblade

virtue with me or you shall regret it." Her hands tightened into fists and she clenched her jaw.

"Ah, the little girl, still trying to be a hero are we?" He chuckled and suddenly his eyes flashed darkly, his countenance becoming horrifying and angry to the beholder. He rose so swiftly, one would have been at odds to say if he had been seated at all before that. His fingers lifted to point accusingly at her, and when he spoke his voice held agony and fury. "We both know you'll never be a hero. You can't even stand before your own town without a mask to hide your face. What made you believe you could stand before me!?" He seemed to grow taller and darker, menace bubbling into his being.

Silver side-stepped in apprehension, but Kim set a firm palm upon his neck to calm the stallion's erratic movement. "What I do is to protect the people," she shot back in anger. How dare he slur her character! But was he not correct?

Vukodlak laughed, icy and cruel. "We both recognize what you do and what you'd *like* to do are two very different things. You'll never serve the people of Ranger's Valley. Your heart is as black as mine. In your mind you've become their protector, their champion, but in reality all you are to them is a thorn. You've realized why my followers pursue them. You know how to stop this, yet you don't."

"For my family then," Kim seethed, her left hand inching toward her hip holsters.

"Your family?!" Vukodlak exclaimed, leering. "You mean that ill-humored Governor Ranger and his laughable group of children?" He shook his head, some of the charming appearance returning to him. "Poor Kim. Even her own father didn't enlighten her with the truth." The creatures and men packed snugly about the ring howled, preparing to leap in and rip her apart should their master give the command.

"What are you saying?" She whispered, confusion gusting across her brow.

"Do you know why your father wanted to leave Ranger's Valley?" He queried, pacing to the steps of the throne. "Because he was afraid." Vukodlak let the words settle on her mind. "He was frightened of me."

Kim observed her foe as he strutted forward haughtily and began to recount the tale. Her throat constricted with each syllable he pronounced, but all were merely blind slaps at a numb heart.

"He knew, Kim. All along he knew about me and my wolf-men. He believed I would return one day to claim the town, the first foothold in regaining my empire. He realized this and was terrified because he knew what I have the power to control. He negotiated a deal with me and signed over his life," the dreadful man sneered. "It was a modest bargain: he would stay on as governor of Ranger's Valley and when I was organized I could merely walk in and take it, allowing him and his pitiful family to go free.

"But he grew anxious. I reason that the old man, Maximus, had filled his head with nonsense and he was finally beginning to believe it. I dispatched a courier with a letter to the governor, describing the horrors that would befall him if he failed me. The puny man got scared, as all men do, and he ran. He thought perhaps if he got far enough away he might escape my wrath. Maybe the thought even crossed his mind of imparting my plans to someone there in the city. I couldn't leave that to chance, now could I?" Vukodlak slowly descended the lopsided stairway.

"I directed my werewolves to chase him down; you were there. You saw them. They did everything I requested of them. All, that is, but one menial task. For some undefinable reason they could not destroy the one person I had most desired them to." His gaze flickered sideways towards her, an expression of near compassion lingering there. "You," he whispered.

Kim's consciousness reeled. Why would it matter so much about killing her? Her father had been the one who'd known all his secrets.

"My warriors slew your supposed family. They hunted you down, but you called sanctuary. So they could not reach you. Though, in the end, they managed to mark you, infecting your very being. Not a complete failure." He rolled his shoulder blades. "You suffered, oh how you suffered these past years." He made a methodical gesture over his lane of travel, the grass once again parting to reveal the stone pathway. He took several measured steps toward her as he spoke. "They were never your

Ranger

family, Kim. They were merely your foster parents, your adopted parents. You were never a Ranger and you won't ever be." He halted halfway between his throne and the white stallion, laughing. "You're my brother's daughter."

Kim's heart thudded in her chest so that she thought it might beat through her bones, but she could feel no sensations. Somehow the dread and the sharp sting of pain had entirely been consumed by her numbness. Though, far down inside something was being fueled: her fury and her rage.

"You're more similar to me than you can ever imagine. We share the same blood, you and I." His pointed boots thumped down on the rock track, generating an echo to his explanation. "You've known this, haven't you? Somehow you grasped the reality that you are the one the legends speak of. You're supposed to be my ruin, my destruction. But how," he threw his hands into the air as if appealing to the firmament, "are you, a girl too frightened of her own identity, supposed to overcome all the darkness in me?

"It would take more light then the sun to wash away the stains of my deeds. And we both know, you don't have a speck of light in you. You're black, just like me. Your soul has been corrupted by the talons of a beast from hell, and darkness floods your mind. Days have been as centuries to you and you've built a wall inside, a shield meant to protect you from your troubled past. But all it succeeds in doing is fetch you nearer to your knees before me.

Admit it, Kim," his voice pulled at the weaving of her inmost core, dragging her will toward his. "You and I are identical. We were born to be something greater than this world could ever comprehend.

"We were not destined to hide in the shadows. We were intended to be recognized and feared, to have power and dominion. And we shall have it!" Vukodlak's path abruptly ended beside Silver. He stretched out a hand to her, his dark eyes shining. "Take my offered gift and we shall rise unto such greatness as the realm has yet to know."

Kim blinked blearily at his indistinct features, her eyelids heavy and her awareness lethargic. Silver snorted in apprehension and shifted his weight as she sat there hesitating.

Like twin vipers striking in the stillness, two explosions detonated, and a pair of creatures collapsed to the dirt, dead. The rest flurried into a panic of motion and howls. Kim's mind jolted awake and her intentions of rescue flooded in. Her plan had been forgotten long ago, but Tonto had arrived and he was acting on his strategy. His matching pistols smoking, he lugged the revolvers both back into their holsters and was at Will's side in a moment, slicing his bonds with a deer-bone knife.

Vukodlak shrieked, his cry shrill as if he were a flacon striking at his prey. The creatures poured into the clearing, swallowing the invader and prisoner amidst their ranks. A single shot cracked off, the Asgaya-wahya freezing in their tracks, saliva spewing between their teeth. "That was a warning,"

Kim shouted, her mount backing up and shaking his ears. "I have more than enough rounds to do serious damage to your men, Vukodlak. Have them stand down and allow us to leave as we are, or countless will die. This I promise you."

At first Vukodlak glared at her, defying the cocked pistol in her hand. Gradually his foul appearance melted and he smiled, waving to dismiss his followers. "Let them go," he ordered coolly. Uncertainly, the shape changers slunk away, a few morphing into men as they stole into the wood.

William tried to stand but his knees buckled. Tonto hastily righted him, slipping a shoulder under the chaplain's arm. Scout pounded into the glade beneath the high overarch of trees, cantering through the outer ring of wolf-men. Tonto called her near, mounting up with Will behind him. They sprinted from the dell, searching for the forest path. Silver backed away slowly, Kim swinging her guns over the Asgaya-wahya bordering her route of escape.

"I'm regretful we had to part in this fashion," Vukodlak raised his cry after her, the attractive manner completely overwhelming his being once more. "A shame having this end so quickly."

Kim snorted, "I'm finding it very agreeable to leave just now." With a prod of her knees the rider and stallion bolted, far from the darkest portion of the forests.

"Run, child. Terror may not be able to touch you, but worse things will haunt you. You'll come running back to me before this is over; I know. You're more comparable to me then you ever could imagine." Vukodlak grinned. The misty, ashen bodies of his deceased faithful blasted into the breeze and churned away into the darkness that consumed him.

Chapter 15

The edge of the timbers was in view, and Kim could make out the forms of her companions on Scout's back just ahead. Horse and rider surged from the tree line in full gallop, but as Kim let the moments in the glade fade into the back of her mind all was unexpectedly overwhelmed in surprise when she was flipped forward over the neck of her mount and tossed into the dirt beyond.

She braced herself on faintly stinging elbows and brushed at her dirt-streaked face. A bruise was forming on her chin and her right arm tingled a little, but that was all.

Why had she been thrown? Kim peered swiftly over her shoulder; Silver had collapsed and was thrashing his forelegs uselessly in the sand. In the rearmost of her awareness she heard Tonto shout out her name. Distantly she perceived the soil spew away from his moccasins as he ran toward her. But all she could focus on clearly was the snowy animal and the crimson liquid that oozed through the dirt all around him. And beneath her numbness she felt. She experienced alarm and hurt and terror.

Somehow Kim succeeded in working her feet under her, jogging back to Silver's side, and somehow she managed to bathe her hands in his warm blood. Tonto was at the horse's dropping-place in seconds and hurriedly inspected him for the wound that had emanated the exuding flow. He towed his buckskin shirt up over his head, wrapping it over an elongated tear in the stallion's quivering rear leg.

Kim's barricades suddenly broke with the rushing tide of sensation. Tears began to course their salty tracks down her cheeks without her consent. She sat with Silver's silky face in her lap, the fluid from her eyes washing the stain of her hands from his hair.

Tonto secured the wrap and straightened, beckoning Scout to himself. William had since dismounted, and stood nearby, uncertain what he ought to do. Tonto's low voice distracted the minister. "I'm going to fetch a friend; he alone can save the horse. Do nothing for it, but," He paused, flipping the reins over his mares ears. "Keep it alive. I shall return in haste." he mounted, kicking dust toward the horizon.

William sensed he needed to do something, if not for the animal then for its rider. Kim lay curled next to the stallion's head, blood and tears trailing over her clothes and hands. Gently Will strode nearer. He hesitated once or twice so as not to alarm her, as certain people in such a state could easily be susceptible to panic. When he'd first met her he'd seen fire in her eyes; a firm, resilient thing that would not easily break. She had been extremely collected, well held together.

But he had also perceived a lack of something, perhaps it was emotion or perhaps it had been some entirely different thing. However, he never believed he would witness her in this manner, and some of her mystery faded away. She was a person, not simply a block of rock with a heart that kept her walking. There was something inside.

A solid stone lodged itself in Kim's throat. It clenched at her air, and she thought she might stop breathing. But the moments continued to drag on, and Kim still lingered there watching Silver's eyes blink lethargically. Her heart felt fatigued; it felt so heavy. Yet there was still a tangible senselessness she could grab onto, a peaceful void far from the screaming of her mind and soul. She snatched after it. Slowly, the cold, numb nothing moved back in. Like a tempest's cloud obstructing the sky, it blanketed her consciousness, the tears faltering and then ceasing. Kim sat, blinking down vacantly at her friend. Her flesh growing chilled against the warm skin of her stallion, and, as if her mind had finally gone to sleep, the world around her went black. The vacant hollowness becoming a reality once more.

Dirt. Moist, brown dirt with little hairy roots forking their small vines this way and that was the first sight Kim beheld. She heaved herself into a sitting position and deftly pushed the animal hide off her knees. Peering about, Kim noted she was in what appeared to be a miniature, underground cave-like excavation. It smelled dank and faintly musty but the rich earthy scent overrode the others. A sun-hardened clay pitcher sat in a similarly fashioned bowl beside the access shaft; otherwise the room was completely bare.

Kim brushed her palms against the close walls as she exited, a few of the tiny, sand grains flaking off with her skin. The tunnel went on for no lengthy amount of time and it opened wide into a larger cavern of lighter colored soil. Tonto, William, and an odd man painted with various hues all sat cross-legged on woven mats in a circle. They each glanced up as she entered, all of them smiling as one.

Kim paced farther in, making her steady way toward them, still uncertain what was happening and what had occurred. Her brain was muzzy and her memory a bit foggy. As she came, Kim twisted her neck to see this remarkable under-earth refuge.

The chamber was plain like the other. Except for the three men, their mats, a few water skins, and a meshed basket of berries, it was empty. Behind the other inhabitance, another passageway curved and sunlight poured in through an opening that must have been just beyond the bend in the shaft.

"Where are we?" She asked, staring at the dyed man who resembled something that looked like an Indian.

"Aye, I don't reckon you to remember," The ancient male with the bright blues and forest greens adorning his face spoke up, pushing himself to his feet. "But you were here once before."

Tonto and William rose as well. "Kim," Her Indian bother interposed, presenting the unusual fellow to her. "This is Rashadi."

Kim's mind stirred. *'Rashadi, Rashadi...'* Ah, yes! he had been the one who'd saved her life after the accident. He'd healed her...well, kept her alive. She bowed her head to the peculiar old man. "Rashasdi, I am in your debt."

"Twice over, it would seem." He chuckled, clasping his wrinkled hands together.

Kim cocked an eyebrow. This under-dweller spoke riddles. "He succeeded in dousing the bleeding and sutured Silver's wound." Tonto explained, beaming. "It seems that your horse has also been injured by the Asgaya-wahya and has likewise survived to share the tale, that of his rider."

Kim nodded, her understanding crystalizing more with each passing moment.

"Come, sit with us." Rashadi offered, gesturing to a fourth mat she'd failed to notice before. "We would much appreciate your practical thoughts."

Kim hesitated but then stepped forward and seated herself, cross-legged, between the timeworn man and Tonto.

"We were just speaking of the day previous," Tonto enlightened her, reseating himself. "Rashadi has an interest in all we've learned. He is deeply eager to understand more about the werewolves so that he might discover a method to cast them away."

Rashadi shook his head, a few feathers pushing through his greying hair. "I do not believe anything can drive them out, nor kill them but for the silver. It seems even old age touches them not, nor hunger, nor loneliness, nor alarm. All that can slay or even harm them would be the metal you carry."

"And what of the individuals who have been damaged by the wolf-men?" Will queried. "Is there no way to cure them of the curse?"

"I have only ever seen two survive the bite an' claw of an Asgaya-wahya," Rashadi replied, reaching into the basket of berries and retrieving an onion from their midst. "This young lady and her horse." He motioned to Kim with the knife he pulled from his leggings. "Though even she shall not be affected by the passage of time. The worries and sensations of this realm may touch them both, but never as severely as it will us mortals. However," He bounced the dear-bone blade in his hand. "She – I cannot say for the horse – will experience a rage and wrath as something deep and rooted within. For that, my friends, is what the wolves feed on.

"Her physical stature altered with the poison, and her strength is terribly frightening if unleashed against you. Pray, don't irk her." He chuckled softly and Kim found she didn't care if they spoke of her. She desired to know all of this as well.

"But then, there is no manner in which she can become…"Tonto sought for the correct word to express his thought. "Un-poisoned? She'll never perish?"

Rashadi began to skin his onion one layer at a time. "The only method I know that could end her fate as she is, half human half beast, is if she were to turn fully into an Asgaya-wahya, or unless her scar was melted away with silver. I don't believe this would have the desired effect however, for you must apply the hot metal to the wound directly and I fear that would destroy the one who was infected."

"So," Kim mused quietly, drawing all of their eyes onto her. "I'll live forever, become a full blooded follower of Vukodlak, or someone will try to restore me. All ways lead to a sort of death."

Rashadi agreed, dipping his chin. "It seems these are the choices that lie before you, now as well as in the future. Existing endlessly would eventually ware away your resolve and you would ultimately turn to Vukodlak, no matter your determination. A being cannot resist something when the heart of it, the actual essence, is inside of them. One day you would cave in."

Kim glanced up at them with a nod. "Sooner or later I know I shall be swayed to his will." Tonto and William's expressions mirrored surprise at her confession. "I almost have already."

"But you're the chosen one. You can't become one of his." Will reasoned, confusion clouding his eyes.

"Why not?" Kim tested, her features relaxed. "Not all legends are true." She sighed, determination setting her jaw. "But I don't intend to let go easily."

Rashadi placed the onion on the mat beside him. "And what do you aim to do, miss? Tonto has told me of your aspiration to hunt the Asgaya-wahya and he also informed me of your venture into the lair of Vukodlak himself. These may be acts of bravery or foolish notions of grandeur; whichever they are you cannot do any good unless you have a plot to follow or a hope for something in the future. I see neither in you." His remark was sorrowful, yet blunt.

Kim bowed her head. Her mind found his words convicting, but all he said was truth. "I've never had a plan. I've not really ever had a purpose for hunting them except to perhaps help me become who I used to be; to stop them from pursuing me. And maybe, at the end, they will cease to terrorize my mind, but now I realize there never will be a tomorrow for me. I am who I am, and nothing can change that unless I die.

"But I do have a strategy, a hope and a belief to fight for." Kim rose, the top of her head nearly brushing the moist cavern's dirt ceiling. Her dark mask remained in place, yet somehow she felt as if she were bearing open her soul for them to see in a way which no one else had ever before been privileged to. "I'm not standing against this swell of evil for myself any longer; there is nothing left to fight for in me. I am black as Vukodlak himself.

"However, I do understand if I choose to lie down, if I drop my guns and allow the monster that I am trying to overcome inside run loose in this time and spread terror over the people, I am far worse than he. For I saw a chance to aid the populaces but I permitted my selfishness to blind me. I perceived a light in the dankness but I tolerated it to be washed out by my own detachment. I held the only weapon that could do any damage and I simply let it go because I didn't consider myself able to hold out in the face of the wickedness that rose. That will not be my memory.

"I recognize I cannot do this on my own, but I do know I am able to do something. That is my proposal; to battle for a purpose that is greater than myself, because I've come to realize I am nothing." She left them sitting there in their thoughts. Tracing though the final shaft and into the bright daylight, Kim breathed deeply the scent of open air. Outside in the green and gold morning a white stallion wandered.

Rashadi proceeded to fish forth another onion, shedding back its flesh. "Your companion is odd, Tonto. The girl has spirit, there can be no doubt. She has courage. You can detect it in her eyes. She holds wisdom and understanding, you hear it when she speaks. But all this is being drowned beneath a torrent of other things. She will proceed with her choices, going about them with hard vigor and you'll be there to see it – most likely being towed along in her wake. Just be wary she does not drag you in the wrong direction." He cautioned. "Sometimes paths and meanings are clouded by false judgment and inside her the father of deceit is growing. Beware."

Chapter 16

"Where's Kim?"

Tonto pivoted, surprised to hear Will's voice behind him. Scout nickered, shaking her mane, and he patted his mare's neck.

"Down the fence line, I believe." He replied, curious as to why the young man had shown up here, in the middle of the night. But maybe he was wondering the same of him and Kim. Tonto huffed in a laugh. Times were strange.

"Thank you." Will nodded his appreciation. Stuffing his hands deep into his coat pockets, he began to follow the fence posts further into the darkness.

"Don't bother her too much," Tonto called after him. "She's in one of those moods." He rolled his eyes and made a cutting motion across his throat.

"Right." Will mumbled under his breath, scanning the area ahead for the individual he sought. Shrouded moonlight shone down in misty blotches from above, reflecting dimly off certain patches of the ground. No other human was in sight and for a moment William wondered if Tonto hadn't meant the other direction.

"What are you doing here?" Kim voice rose from the shadows behind him and Will started both from the suddenness of the sound and by how he could have missed her, even in the vague light.

The minister turned, supposing he'd find her scowling into his face; she was nowhere to be seen. "I came to speak with you. I had a few thoughts I desired to share." He glanced about, probing for her with his eyes as he spoke.

"Just keep your volume low; we're expecting company." Kim instructed. She shifted her boot slightly and Will finally perceived her. Garbed in all black, she was difficult to spot pressed up against the fence and half obscured behind a bale of old straw. She looked prepared for a ground assault, which was exactly what she was waiting for.

Will squatted down, feeling a bit peculiar hulking over her, and swept his gaze over the exposed field of corn stubble. "What makes you think they'll come?" He questioned, the tranquil breeze washing over him.

She lifted her left hand to rest on the horizontal fence board, a pistol in her other palm. Dark blue eyes roamed the arena. "Because I'm here, and they want me dead."

He pursed his lips. "True. But did you ever wonder why?" Will balanced on his toes, clasping his hands together, elbows resting on his knees.

"I suppose because Vukodlak considers me to be the fable child. And I presume they're after me because they never have finished what they started." She flexed her jaw, feeling the same deep-rooted tightness in her left cheek.

"Have you yet stopped to consider there might be a reason behind why Vukodlak's wolf-men haven't completed the task? Why they didn't kill you with the rest of the governor's family?" Kim caught how he said the *governor's* household, not hers.

She shrugged indifferently. "What's there to think about? I outran them and they missed their chance, that's all."

"Is it?" Will eased into a more comfortable position. "For me it's a little hard to imagine them being outpaced and I'm convinced they don't just *miss* their target. And you most certainly were their objective that night."

Kim heaved an irritated sighed. "Did you come to ask about my past, or to aggravate me about my future? This is a dangerous place for certain people right now. It might be prudent if you left." She stared out into the dusky haze that was gathering over the field's vacant expanse.

"I shall leave, but not quite yet. I have a few additional questions which will inevitably lead me to my point for coming in the first place." Silence issued forth like a thick blanket. Kim refused to so much as twitch. William picked up the conversation again, whispering his next enquiry, "Have you ever thought that maybe you prevailed over your lethal injury because you had a role to play in the history to come? Because it was God's purpose to use you in accomplishing His victories here?"

Kim snorted, pulling her hand away from the fence to fiddle with the revolver's rounds. "You sound like Maximus," She muttered.

"Well," Will smirked. "He did teach me the grander portions of what I know. But, honestly Kim, do you seriously consider it only a coincidence? Look at all the factors and how they fell into place; the discovering of that clearing, the wolves being unable to penetrate into you. Tonto's being there that night to aid you. Really?"

She shrugged, pushing the cylinder of her pistol out and sending it spinning. "Life is overflowing with weird happenings. I guess I'm just one of the stranger ones."

Will shook his head sadly. "How can you say that? Look around you! Everything you perceive is no accident." He rose, straightening his cramping legs. "Back in the home of Rashadi, you pronounced you were nothing. Obviously you must then consider something or someone as greater than yourself."

Kim slapped the pistol together, slamming it into her opposite hand. She clenched it tightly, her knuckles turning white.

"God has a calling on your life. You might not realize it yet; you may have to go through hell itself to understand it, but He's calling you, Kimberly Ranger. He wants you, and He will have no other." William tucked his hands inside his coat and strode along the fence line.

He passed by Tonto with a simple nod. "Hunt well. She seemed a bit distracted. Watch her back."

Tonto nodded, slightly amazed the chaplain didn't have an irate Kim hounding his footsteps.

"Fifth night out here," He scuffed his moccasin though the dirt. "I doubt we'll spot anything."

Will mounted his borrowed mare. Urging her into a trot, he wheeled their heads toward town and disappeared into the twilight. Tonto's mind briefly supposed that they should have allowed the young man to stay with them; might have been safer, though it was too late now. Hopefully he would reach the settlement swiftly and have the good sense to stay indoors. They hadn't seen anything more than a desolate corn field the previous evenings, but that could change quickly.

Tonto absently rechecked his firearm. It was still as fully loaded and ready to go as it been the prior times he'd fiddled with it. He flipped the revolver about in his dark hand, wondering how well he could actually shoot it during a skirmish. Kim had practiced with him, but not nearly as much as he would have preferred. She could pick a fly off a horse's nose with either pistol. He, on the other hand, still required a bit of training.

A fleeting shadow sped across the distant backdrop and he thought perhaps there had been a flash of crimson accompanying it. Tonto settled his gun into the rawhide holster on his belt and leaned forward with his elbows on the board fence, his eyes narrowing as he scanned the area. There was definitely something out there in the gloom. His right hand slipped back down to the pistol's butt and he latched on, waiting to pull it loose.

A vacant howl resonated out across the widespread expanse, and from the distance they came running. They hurled themselves onward with all the strength in their massive bodies and rushed headlong toward the boundary of posts.

Tonto's hands moved as he had taught them, swinging the twin pistols out from their resting places and leveling one at the leaping beasts. A shot rang out louder than rumbling thunder, and one of the creatures staggered and fell; Kim was already on the move.

Tonto sighted down the short barrels, one at a time, and fingered the triggers in turn. The small guns cracked in report, sending up smoke and jolting his arm backward slightly. He cocked both revolvers simultaneously with either of his thumbs and took aim once more.

Farther down the fence stood Kim, firing off several shots when any one of the creatures came within range. Presently, her first couple of pistols had run out of rounds. She spun them into their holsters, speedily removing the next two so as to continue her wall of defense. At some point, she'd have to cease her barrage to replenish each of her guns. How was Tonto doing this with only a pair of pistols?

From behind her position, Kim sensed a hostile presence. She spun on her heels and blasted a wolf as it dove toward her, its mouth wide and gapping. The creature dropped lifeless at her feet, and she swallowed hard. A clawed hand winged passed her hat, and Kim backed away from the fence line, discharging shot after shot into the masses. "Tonto!" She hollered, spinning the cartridge open on her firearms. "I'm out!"

"Got it!" He returned in a shout. His own pistols blazing with loud retorts, he marched backward until their shoulders met and they both paused. Kim yanked the silver bullets from the gun belts that were mounted over her chest and stomach, slamming them into the cylinder as quickly as her fingers would allow. The process was slow and methodical; a few of the bullets slipped from her grasp in her haste and fell to the dirt.

"I'm full." She finally called, stepping away slightly and letting the closest wolves have a taste of her metal. There were so many. How could Vukodlak afford to lose them?

Abruptly, the world fell into silence, and Kim checked herself, swiftly glancing around. The creatures had backed off, vanishing into the murky night. Was that it then? Were they to win so easily? She greatly mistrusted this sudden retreat. Kim hastily restocked her revolvers, taking out all four pistols to reload.

"They're going to be back." Tonto muttered, twisting his bullet-filled belts so the remaining ammunition was in front. "Regrouping, reforming their strategy, I don't know, but I don't like it." He whispered, examining the shadows. Scout danced toward them, her ears twitching. Tonto reached out to pat her on the neck. "Steady girl," He spoke comfortingly. "You're safe." She quietened, but her eyes still shone white in the moonlight.

Kim slid her revolvers into their rawhide sheaths and inhaled deeply, waiting. "Whatever the purpose behind their sporadic attack, Vukodlak must have decided he didn't require quite as many of the Asgaya-wahya for his design as he thought. He would have never been able to afford losing this many before. I wonder what it is he plots."

"We could ask him." Tonto sniffed, half jesting.

"We might have to do that." Kim remarked flatly. "But I'd prefer not to." Her right firearm rose up as the words passed her lips. She set it off and Tonto swallowed as a werewolf crumpled to the ground behind him. She let the smoking barrel fall to her side. "If you can, try to take one of these pawns alive. There are some very interesting questions I'd like to ask them."

"Sure." Tonto agreed, somewhat shaken. Palming his gun, he about faced and stealthily duck-ran to the straw bundle that lay next to the fence row. He took up a position alongside the make-shift shelter and paused, waiting for the foul beasts to show themselves.

Kim scuttled off into the shadows, praying the gloom would shield her from any unseen enemies that prowled nearby. She slunk behind the only scraggly tree within miles, and listened, her pistols cocked and ready for the onslaught.

The hush grew thicker, and Kim's mind felt as if the quiet was attempting to suffocate her.

Gradually, her eyes readjusted into night vision, and she found Tonto's location nearer to the fence, beside the straw pile some farmer had discarded there ages ago. The pitiable mound was riddled with mildew, and the twine that had bound it together had altogether disintegrated. Rain had saturated its grasses, snow had buried it, but still the heap endured to lean upon the fence posts, outlasting time itself, it seemed. Kim knew her life would be like those bales if she did nothing for it; loose, left behind, and fallen apart to last for eternities.

Kim caught the sound of a pistol cocking and glanced toward Tonto; he must have seen something. But her brother hadn't stirred, not even his hair blew in the wind. She narrowed her eyes and scanned the field without moving her head. Her cheek flamed suddenly, and Kim swung around to the loud clap of a shot being fired. The huge man she'd met in town her second day, and later who'd also been so hostile to William, stood leering at her, the pistol smoking in his hand.

Kim could feel the warm blood gushing down her shoulder and over her arm. She could sense the slightest stab of pain in her flesh; the bullet had passed straight through. Her eyes shifted from her shoulder to his face, her features fierce with defiance.

"Nice try," Kim spat, her right hand inching to her hip holster. "But that's not how you kill a werewolf." In a flash, she had the gun out and ready. A puff of smoke and silver light followed as it went off. The giant wolf-man howled like a wild hound, crumping to the ground and clutching at his hand.

She glared disdainfully down at him, suffering in the filth, and brushed at her blood-soaked shirt sleeve; the wound in her upper arm had sealed over already. He hadn't the courage to carry silver on his person, and she couldn't die by standard weapons. Crouching down next to the Asgaya-wahya, Kim scowled at him. "Tell me, why does your master permit you and your companions to run into a fire fight without any defense? Why can he afford to lose you? What does he want?"

The man coughed, his eyes glazing over. He groped at her with the hand she'd shot. Kim's eyes grew. The flesh on his fingers had begun to crystalize and turn an ashy-grey color. Slowly the transformation climbed up his arm. "Master desires..." His nose twitched and his appearance began to morph into that of a startled wolf-creature. "He wants you." He gasped a final breath and then was no more.

Kim exhaled and straightened, the dust of her former foe wafting away into the night. She already knew Vukodlak sought her soul; he'd told them as much. She kicked the dirt and landed her hands on her hips. No other werewolves rose from the gloom. Not a single one remained to contest with them that night. This last challenger had been the test.

Tonto darted over, blue eyes wide and shining white on his dark face. "What happened?" He queried, lightly touching her shoulder where the bullet had pierced through, tearing her clothing and staining it crimson. "I heard two shots."

"We're done for the night." She refused his question, slinging her gun away. "Pack it in." Kim turned and started homeward, a white stallion greeting her on the trail.

Tonto watched her go, uncertain exactly what had transpired. Another round had been fired besides Kim's; the pistol lay at his feet near the tree, its barrel still hot. But no other evidence remained. Even her wound had vanished.

He hefted the firearm from the ground into his hand, staring at it. Tucking it into his belt, Tonto jogged over to Scout and mounted up. "Let's go," he whispered, and she took off into the night.

Chapter 17

It haunts me. I've known for some time I was a werewolf, and I know I can't be killed by any material except silver. But it disturbs me to actually witness it. To experience it. My shoulder doesn't even hurt any longer. For a while, there was a dull ache, but now there's nothing. Just a scar and a tattered shirt. The worst part is, I can never change from who I am. There is no hope for me. There will be no future. Only a now and a later. Just a lone Ranger without a family and without a plan.

I realize what I have to do. I've understood since I first learned about all of this. But how to go about it when I know I'm not nearly strong enough to achieve my so called destiny? No one can support me, because no one understands; Tonto can't for he isn't like me and William just carries it all back to God. I can't even help myself, for I am nothing.

Even if God were real – as Will likes to believe – even if He cared about people, why would He bother with me? I'm not a person; I'm not even a wolf. I'm something in-between, and somehow, I think that must be worse than either extreme. How can He have a design for my life? I don't have a life. I merely exist, that's all. I breathe, and my heart beats, barely. I highly doubt this was how God intended anyone to live. Or am I even alive? I've come to ask that question numerous times. Shouldn't I feel something, anything? Or am I just the existing dead? Fated to walk this earth in numb isolation, cut off from the outside world? Is this who I am? I pray it might not be so. Nay, I beg it. But I know I cannot change, for I am that which I am.

"Have you seen the damage they did to the town?" William asked. His face was beet-red, and he gasped for breath. The minister doubled over in the middle of the forest track to pant in more air. He had just arrived from Ranger's Valley, bearing news of the weighty disorder that had broken out there.

Kim growled and clenched her fist. Their trivial effort to keep the Asgaya-wahya far from the people and the settlement had simply been a set up. Vukodlak had dispatched his fiends to do their filthy work, so that while Tonto and she had been busy routing the alleged *herds* the remainder had been devastating the town. She grasped her belt, staring straight ahead. "How many taken? How much damage done?"

"I'm not positive who all was seized, but for sure one young man has been reported missing, and a handful were found slain." He paused out of grief.

"Everyone else is accounted for?" Tonto probed.

Will nodded. "Those lost were being properly taken care of when I left. As for the damage to the town, I think it's something better observed than explained." He let his words rest and stepped out of their path. "I must return now. They'll be needing me to say the burial rights." He bobbed his head in farewell and began walking back, jumping into a sprint further up the trail.

Tonto's hand fell heavily upon his mare's neck as he stroked her. "At times I find myself wondering why we even bother." He grunted, casting his gaze into the timbers. "We do our best and try our hardest for what's right or things we believe should be fought for, and all we accomplished was for naught.

"Every ounce of sweat we mustered didn't stop them from slaughtering at least a dozen people and wrecking the settlement. How is that justifiable? What's the point of protecting when what you're trying to defend is never the precise thing that needs shielding at the time?" He tossed his hands up in exasperation.

"I reckon we should go see it." Kim spoke quietly, acknowledging the fact that they were somewhat responsible for the destruction that was done.

"Why? What can we do for them now?" He huffed, patting Scout's neck more profusely. "We're too little too late."

"I expect it is a bit late for the town and for the poor folks who died, but maybe there is something we can do. Perhaps if we simply let them have hope that we're fighting for them."

"How are they supposed to have confidence if you don't even have it!?" His countenance looked a tad heated, and instantly he regretted his outburst. "I'm sorry." He muttered. "I'm just exhausted because there doesn't seem to be an end."

Kim observed Tonto out of the corner of her eye. He had always been the one to hold his head high, to keep his spirits up, and he carried the bulk of her burdens. He was no broken wreck like she was. And yet, there he sat, crushed and regretful. Inside, he was a mess just like her; he simply knew how to disguise it.

Kim prodded Silver up next to Scout. She reached across the gap between them, touching his shoulder lightly. "We do have hope," she corrected, though she didn't quite believe it herself. Kim let her hand slip away, asking Silver to move on.

Tonto knew she didn't put stock in what she said, but his heart surged. He would simply have to trust in it for her. "Come on, girl," he whispered, giving Scout a last resounding pat on the shoulder and nudging her ahead.

Ranger's Valley was worse off than either Kim or Tonto could have imagined. The hitching posts lay ripped from the soil and strewn about the earthen road. The few porches outside businesses and homes that were significant enough to warrant railings had them no longer. Claw marks, bullet holes, and blood decorated several outer walls of structures. Some shops even had their overhanging roofs ripped down to litter the streets and block the doorways.

Gatherings of people congregated in ragtag groups by the governor's — who had also doubled as the sheriff — old home. Most were menfolk but a few women and children hung about the edges, apprehensive thoughts creasing their foreheads.

As the two dark riders came loping into town, dust roiling in clouds about their mount's hooves, the murmuring quieted, and all eyes turned toward them. Kim sensed every face in the throng focusing on her. She could read from their eyes the respect and fear they held for her, their lips beginning to whisper the name they'd heard from the minister. One would nudge his neighbor and they'd share a significant glance, until it had circulated throughout the entire assembly.

Kim pulled Silver up before the rows of individuals, her gaze flittering over their heads. "Can anyone tell me the name of the one who was taken? And are there any others not marked among the deceased who still remain missing?" She spoke commandingly, taking stock of their frazzled situation. William was not among the masses. Doubtless, he was still with the mourners, praying over the burial.

The hum of voices rose and fell but nothing audibly clear was verbalized. A lean, wrinkled farmer set a foot forward, his sun-bleached, straw hat clamped in his hands. He appeared nervous, unsure where to leave his eyes. He finally decided on the ground.

"They took me brother's son," his feeble voice choked up. He ran the hat's brim in circles through his fingers. "He were only a boy, small and scrawny to look at." His eyes grew wide and he peered at her face, betrayal written in the puckers of his tanned brow. "It weren't no animal that took 'im, 'ner. Twas a man."

Several of the females gasped, a few men nodded, and one or two proclaimed: "Aye, I saw 'im."

Silver stomped at a fly by his hoof and snorted. "Your senses do not deceive you," Kim replied, speaking generally to all. "There are men among their ranks. Though to many of you they may appear as ones you had once believed to be your friends. Do not let yourselves be misled. They are your enemy. And they will kill you." Her words were firm and to the point, leaving no wiggle room.

Tonto straightened beside her; they were the hope of the people.

"Be wary," Kim warned, Silver beginning to back away. "Some may even be amongst you now. Concealed in the guise of a lamb is that of a wolf ever waiting to deceive. Watch and discern wisely." She tossed the old farmer a single silver bullet. "Only those with a pure heart will be willing to hold that without distress. I suggest permitting everyone to grasp it." She peeled away from the throng, setting her course for the north.

"Where da you go?" The people's spokesman questioned.

Ranger

Kim called over her shoulder, her auburn hair wafting in the breeze. "I go to confront the devil; Vukodlak shall answer for the deeds of his followers. I go to bring back hope." Silver bolted across the road, Scout not far behind.

The collection of grave diggers had returned from the burial site, catching view of the hazy dust cloud racing away. The timeworn man fingered the silver shot in his hand as his brother straggled up behind him. Planting the dented shovel in the ground, he leaned heavily upon it. "Who were that?" He jerked his head in the direction of the fleeing horses.

The elderly farmer placed his bedraggled hat back to rest on his head, looking out over the bloodied streets. "The lone Ranger."

Chapter 18

Dark clouds rolled in overhead, blotting out the mid-morning sunlight from the wooded footpath. Silver darted in-between the mossy-carpeted trees and surged ahead in the general direction Kim had journeyed when following Vukodlak's two emissaries.

Soft pellets of rain began to pelt into her hat and roll off the hefty fabric. Washing over Silver in streaks, the water staining him a dull grey color.

Rapidly, the drops increased in size and hailed down around them harder and faster. Kim drew Silver up short, Scout and Tonto nearly colliding with them from the rear.

Tonto squeezed his mare up alongside her, his face shedding rainwater from his nose, chin and eyelashes. "What is it?" He wondered, inquiring why they'd halted so suddenly. He had to shout somewhat to be heard above the rain's substantial dribble on the leaves and loud, rhythmic drumming in their ears.

"I'm not sure which way we go," she replied, casting water off her hat in sheets as she swung her head about, searching.

"Straight on, I think," he explained, pointing off into the woodland. "It looks dimmer up there to me, perhaps the edge of his domain?"

"Possibly." Kim nodded, but she didn't click her mount into motion. "Tonto," She said presently, her words softer. "What do I do if," she paused, thinking. "What if he overwhelms me and I fail?

What will happen to Ranger's Valley and all the inhabitance there if I cannot stand against him?"

To Tonto's eyes she looked once more like the small girl he had found dying in a glade, drenched and dripping as she was, and maybe even fearful. "I don't honestly know," he said, irritated that he couldn't be her solid support in that instant. "But if you fall, no one else will stand. You're their only hope, Kim.

"I don't think I can do this. I don't even comprehend how I'm to go about overcoming Vukodlak in the first place. Silver isn't the answer; he's not a wolf-man. I don't have the words to say or the feelings to express. I don't have anything."

William hurried into his cluttered side-room, shutting the thin, wooden door behind him and bolting it. He needed to be alone right now, uninterrupted by the cares that assailed him beyond this cubicle. His responsibility for the burials had been accomplished, and the rest of the cleanup was underway – led by several respectable and sturdy men. He had a more important task to undertake now.

Will pushed aside a stack of books on the floor with his boot and knelt down near the low table. His head raised skyward, he clasped his hands. He quieted his spirit and came into the presence of the Most High. Someone needed his prayers right now, requiring the support and strength of Him who alone could save her. And all of them.

"So soon do we meet again? Perhaps we should have never parted." Vukodlak rose from his throne in a receiving gesture of his guests. Kim descended from Silver's back, choosing to stand by the stallion's neck this time. Tonto, too, dismounted and held Scout's harness in his darkly tanned hands.

The creatures and men about the expanse growled, bearing their teeth and distaste at the unwise pair.

Lying prone at the feet of Vukodlak's chair was the young lad who had been snatched. He appeared to be unconscious, yet he still breathed.

Kim clenched her jaw. "I have come seeking penance," she stated with confidence. "Recompense for the guiltless lives you stole, for the homes you wreaked, for the innocence that was lost because of you."

The villain laughed, scorning her accusations. "What blameless lives? I saw only individuals caught up in their own covetous desires. What homes? There were merely shops and businesses. What purity?" He narrowed his eyes. "There is no such thing in this world."

"I look around me and observe beings whose existences you devastated. I peer into the eyes of your followers and I see imprisoned souls awaiting liberation. I perceive a slave within them, but I also see a freedom." Kim dropped her hand from Silver's side. "The businesses you saw were not only just that, but families' livelihoods, their way of life. A shed in your mind, a palace in theirs." She took several steps forward. "And yes, there is innocence; it is our children. Things they should not have to know before they are old enough to bear such burdens have been thrown upon them even now. An inner darkness they perhaps did not yet understand existed, but now they have proof of it running wild in the streets." She stood at the base of his throne, glaring up into his eyes.

Vukodlak smirked, waving her arguments aside. "Such eloquence. Alas, all untrue. There has been evil in the world since the beginning. Even you must admit that, blind as you are. My faithful were never captives; they offered themselves freely as all who desire to wield power will. You too shall give yourself fully to this servitude. You already have in certain ways.

"The darkness is in your soul; it's been seeping in for years now, suffocating your passions, willing you to die. You've sensed it, haven't you? It's a cold, impassive numbness. A place within where you consider yourself to be safe, a hole in which to lose your sorrows. And it's anger." He slowly, painstakingly marched down the steps.

His feet an echo to his words as he came to challenge her face to face. "It's thrilling to feel again. After the emotionlessness, a festering hatred and a strength will surge. You can control anything, but you have to embrace it full on."

Kim didn't break his intense stare. "You're right, I have suffered. I've felt it, the darkness leaching into my inner being and choking my heart. I hold onto my numbness as a blissful solace from the agony of feeling and remembering. " She shook her head. "But I don't believe I want the kind of power you speak of."

He smirked. "Always pretending to be the virtuous youth. After you've experienced what I can take away from you, you'll be more than happy to embrace this darkness." He sniffed, and re-ascended his throne. "Tie her to the stake." He ordered indifferently.

"Stay back!" Tonto threatened, flipping a pistol into his hands and sighting down the barrel at the few men who'd stepped inward.

"No, Tonto," Kim decried, glancing over her shoulder at him. "Let them take me. I need to do this. Free the boy, return him to his family." She dipped her head at the lad near her boots.

Her brother swallowed, his aim drooping a little. His eyes saddened and his heart was burdened that he could not do this for her. The wolf-men moved in, while several others fetched a lofty, wooden pole and rammed it deeply into the ground.

"Lash her tightly." Vukodlak instructed. He seated himself, crossing his legs and intertwining his spindly fingers. His face displayed no emotion whatsoever, the lines of his mouth relaxed beneath empty eyes.

Two of the Asgaya-wahya took Kim by either arm and led her to the spike. Her gaze traveled up

Ranger

the length of the pole to the very top. It extended high above them and was stained with blood and other unpleasant things. She lifted an eyebrow, allowing them to push her spine against the stake and loop dirty, coarse rope around her, binding her arms to her sides and her body to the shaft.

Tonto tentatively maneuvered to the unconscious boy's side; the gun still in his hand. Vukodlak shot him a glare but waved the Indian on; there was no longer any need for either of them. Tonto scooped the youth into his arms and darted over to his nervously prancing mare. He hefted the boy onto Scout and, uncertain if he should linger or depart, peered back at the unfolding scene.

Vukodlak had risen, pacing down the uneven steps. The high grass separated to create a pathway for him to advance toward the stake. The wolf-men slipped from the clearing, their work completed. Vukodlak circled her, his hands clasped behind his back.

"We call this pole the stake." He explained. "They used to burn convicted witches on logs such as this, but we're not going to set you on fire. No, we have a much more refined method of going about our practices. However, they tell me the flames would be far easier to endure than that which I'm about to administer on you." He ceased his turning before her, forged pity layering over his other emotions. "I dare say I've never experienced it."

"I'm willing to trade places," Kim grunted, her fingers running along the rough knots.

He chuckled. "Still playing the strong, determined heroine, ever to the final round. You are, truly, resilient. If you're lucky, that may not last, and you'll die swiftly. Yet, I believe you shall survive this, to the very, bitter end. Suffering most dreadfully, I'm sure. But it can all be forgotten in the twinkling of a moment. Simply allow yourself to freely join us." He turned a cold shoulder. "Remember that; you need only be willing to let go."

Kim's brow furrowed in defiance. "Being forced into a choice is not free will."

"Some deem it thus. But presently you will be eager, and quite of your own accord, to bind your spirit to darkness. Shall we begin?"

Kim dipped her chin in consent and tried to quiet her beating heart. She needed to be calm in order to withstand this. She surveyed Vokodlak as he stretched his hands out toward her, mere inches from her face. He closed his crimson eyes, as if concentrating, and exhaled heavily.

Kim didn't know where to set her gaze. At first she examined her enemy's face, so motionless it appeared as though he had expired standing there. She then shifted to peer at the wolves and men; they each glared wrath upon her, some with leers of wicked delight. Tonto had turned his back, draping his arms over the unmoving lad laid out upon Scout. She peeked at her hands and flexed her fingers. Her eyes shifted, taking in the woodland about them, for the trees had begun to groan. It seemed as if everything was bending at an angle toward her and Vukodlak. As if he had fixed all his willpower upon her and every entity under his command was likewise against her. Kim shut out the world then, and focused on peace.

At first Kim felt nothing save the dull, throbbing numbness and the underlying rage that constantly seemed to be in her. She probed through the dense fog of her mind for the tranquility she so desperately desired to hang onto, but it was nowhere to be found.

Steadily, though, a sensation nibbled away at the bottom of her awareness, beginning to thread its path upward, thawing the frozen emotions. Things she'd held back and dumped into the void began to surface. She couldn't shove them away; they just kept coming, stronger than ever before.

First the fear rolled up, pulling her breath away and sucking her thoughts dry. She gasped for air and found herself forcefully panicking. Her fingers clawed at the bindings that held her taut but she couldn't get loose. Her eyes burst wide open and she screamed from her gut. Fright surged over her face in spasms and her heart-rate skyrocketed.

Kim thrashed, lurching her limbs in shuddering jerks and twisting her neck at odd angles. But she was secured far too firmly against the tree to do anything.

Extreme fury overwhelmed her panic, boiling up like a raging fire and threatening to destroy all common sense. Kim's consciousness blanked. With all thoughts of rationality erased, she felt like an unstoppable, furious monster. Guttural cries tore from her throat. Her cheek felt as if it were set ablaze, her entire face being consumed.

Vaguely she perceived the blood that leaked from her scar. It dribbled slowly down her neck and wormed its way beneath her clothing. Kim shook her ropes, tearing at the wooden stake, fuming that they had the audacity to confine her in this fashion.

Steadily, the senseless rage passed, replaced with a furious knowledge, the understanding that her rival was toying with her mind, preying upon her passions. He had removed the barrier that blocked all the uninvited sensations. How dare he.

An awful aching sorrow plagued her next; she felt lost and utterly alone, left to die by herself in the dreadful place, her enemies looking on and gloating in satisfaction. Tears of shame and bereavement flooded her eyes. Kim squeezed her lids shut to keep them back, but they escaped anyhow. She bit her lip, catching a sob before it could break lose. Her inner core trembled, and her mind bent.

Pain streaked suddenly into her hazy, muddled awareness, as all emotion ceased its deluge upon her. She peeled open her eyes; Vukodlak withdrew his hands, pulling them back like spring-coils waiting to be released – the trees and wind bending with him. He held for half an instant, then pushed toward her again with speed and ferocity. Everything exploded into her with a might unknown.

Kim's backbone arched against the pole. Her breath was sucked away so that the shriek building up inside of her could go nowhere. Her mouth gapped open in unfilled silence. Kim's hands went limp and her body protested as her insides were twisted, the agony more extreme than anything she had ever experienced.

But more than the torture, she sensed a shifting of herself. She felt isolation from everything else, even from her own spirit. She was lifeless and alone, cold and frozen, left to linger in a realm of absolute corruption and suffering forever. There was nothing here, no other presence, no light and no darkness; just the scorching all-consuming pain that blanketed her body.

Somehow the emptiness seemed like the epitome of what she had been living, though now it was tangible. Kim had let no one in. She had bottled up her emotions and buried them behind a wall. She'd lost hope and lost desire. It was like she was in one of Reverend Maximus's lessons, one of those cut off from God and all the blessing He gave. Was this what hell was like?

Her consciousness flickered in and out. Fragments of memories and recollections emerged through the agonizing window of red that had occupied her vision: parts of her childhood, and all she'd learned, teachings her mother had pressed upon her even at a young age. Maybe she did need God as William had said. Perhaps He could defeat Vukodlak, or maybe He couldn't. Maybe no one could.

A tremor shook her and Kim fell limp under her bonds. She cried out weakly, whimpering softly. Perhaps the time had come to ease her suffering, to give herself freely. She was breaking, mentally and physically.

Chapter 19

Out of the swirling, red mist that clouded her sight, Kim thought she perceived a faint and distant light. Her eyes continued to bleed tears, her body jerking and shivering with convulsions. Nonetheless, she kept her gaze fastened on the bright spark as it drew ever nearer. The brilliance grew and increased, shimmering in an abnormal liquid light. In her mind she stretched a hand out to it, and reviving warmth flooded into her frigid form with welcoming heat.

"'Reach back to Me. Take My hand, as I offer it freely. Though it be pierced and wounded, it was for you that I suffered; so that you would never have to be separated from the Father."' The Spirit in the midst of the glow spoke, floating toward her. *"'Receive My Spirit. Gain the strength to do My will. Allow Me to cover your past and your future with My blood. For I have accepted the penalty you so merit upon Myself.'"* The radiance enveloped her, and a glimmering golden splendor filled her wide eyes.

The pain and misery melted away as she was entirely cloaked within the Light. Kim welcomed it, bowing her heart in final submission. She'd been bought and paid for; she didn't have to go through the utter separation because He'd already fulfilled the penalty for her. And Kim felt, not in ache or fury; she felt no terror and no grief. What she sensed was limitless joy and absolute peace, a profound love and an infinite hope that spirited her on.

Kim opened her eyes. The rain still poured down from the heavens into her face and her scar still bled, but the internal anguish had ceased. So too the numbness that had haunted her for so long was wiped from within. The frozenness had practically consumed her; it had been her obsession for so long that Kim believed she would never feel in a positive way again. Now it was gone, washed away in a cleansing tide.

The trees swayed back to their normal, upright positions. The wind changed direction and the rain sailed passed her to whip into Vukodlak, his arms still stretched out toward her and his eyes closed. Kim tugged on her ropes; they held just as tight as before. The wolf-men about the perimeter each gaped at her, unsure if they beheld a ghost. A single creature dashed forward, a horrible snarl on its face. The beast bayed once, cowering around her in a wide circle, daring not to get close.

Vukodlak blinked as water pelted into his face. He dropped his hands, noting the shift in the timbers and wind. He snarled. "You are resistant, but not that impervious. You shall break." He lifted a single hand, blue sparks dancing through his fingers. He hurled a pulse of exploding light at her. It flushed over Kim, surrounding her being; warping around her, it dissipated into the air beyond.

Now," Vukodlak said, a smug expression on his face. "Will you give yourself freely?"

"Explain to me what is free about any of this?" She returned. Kim stared intently at him, her question genuine.

"Defiance!" He shouted in anger, fury coloring his expression.

"Irreverence," she countered, giving name to his actions. "Everything we see, all we are, has to be paid for. Nothing is free. I cannot offer myself unto you, for I am not my own. Nothing I am is mine to give." She raised her hands as best she could within the confines of restricted movement. "I gave myself to someone else."

Vukodlak's eyes flashed with ire, and he snapped the crimson cloak down. He seethed through his teeth, spitting venom. "No being but I can control souls here in my realm. There is no power superior to my own in this land. You speak deceit."

Kim smiled with the knowledge of a truth he could not understand. "But there is an authority greater than you. And no matter where I am, It's constantly nearby. You can't fight It, you cannot extinguish It, and you cannot sway It. It dwells within me, so that I too shall not be persuaded by your deceptions."

"Lies," he fumed, stalking toward his throne and collecting himself. He was slowly seated, his countenance once again placid. "No matter. If I can't persuade you to turn, I shall break you. It's your choice." He motioned two of the Asgaya-wahya inward; they both clasped flaming torches and held them high. "You see," He began to explain. "As I said before, they used to burn witches at the stake – fire all about in a ring, no way to get out. You must be a sorceress, to resist my influence. Therefore, we shall dispose of you."

Kim kept her mouth sealed tightly, choosing not to say a word. She surveyed her enemies as they scrapped the flames through the tall grass around her stake, unable to muster enough courage to get closer. She wiggled faintly, the ropes relaxing about her stomach.

"Light her up," Vukodlak instructed, fluttering a hand as if dismissing her. "Dead legends are false hopes."

The creatures moved in, tossing their burning branches at Kim's wet feet, the rain threatening to put them out. But a spell had been placed over the torches and as the torrents collided with the fire, it only intensified and surged higher. The heat flushed up and over Kim's body but she sensed no warmth, only a cool wind. The flames dried her sodden clothing but did not touch her skin or eat through the fabric. Her bonds burnt, seared away by the intense fire and slipped to the ground as papery ash. Kim stepped from the fire, treading her way through the wet weeds. Her eyes glowed brightly out from her dark mask.

"Vukodlak, don't you know legends often hold a grain of truth in them? That's what makes them so believable. Though I cannot defeat you on my own, God can work through me to overcome you."

"Not with my powers! No one can overthrow me." He leaned forward, his hands clenching the throne's armrests. "You can cast me out but I always return, stronger than ever before. Your father couldn't best me. What makes you think you can? Ye of lesser blood then he and far less noble by all rights." he snorted into the damp breeze. "I will not be pushed around by the words of a coward who hides behind a guise. You are pathetic." He glared hatred into her dried face.

"Yes," Kim nodded her agreement. "I am wretched. But that's how He uses me, so that I may not boast it was I who accomplished what He alone can do. Surrender." She set her feet firmly, a shoulder width apart.

"To whom?" He sneered. "A little girl attended by her whims and fancies? I think not. I fought and bleed for my place in this world, and I'm not about to give that up." He flung the dampened cape behind his arm.

"I'm no longer a *little* girl thanks to your werewolves. I'm not so small or so weak. I'm actually quite strong, and I'm not on my own anymore." She elevated her hands, palms pointed toward him, matching his stance.

He smiled wickedly. "Someone will suffer. Maybe it won't be you, but someone always has to suffer."

"No," Kim shook her head. He smirked and deep in her gut a sinking feeling throbbed. She cut her eyes back and forth around the glade; the men and wolves had vanished, every single one.

Vukodlak laughed harshly. "It's too late now. They'll be in the town by this time, and once I've finished with you, Ranger's Valley will be mine. My foothold to a grander glory." A pulse of light surged into Kim's face.

Scout dashed through the trees and on toward the settlement. Tonto couldn't see the Asgaya-wahya but he knew they were behind him. They were coming. After Kim had been tied to the stake, he'd observed the beasts begin to slink away, sneaking out little by little, and had guessed their intentions. He urged his mount to fly faster, charging through the woodland walks while clinging tightly to an unconscious lad. They bounded into the clear, the town within sight. But somehow the beasts had managed to get there ahead of him. It appeared as though the creatures had forced the citizens to retreat into the saloon and the men had barricaded the entrance for protection, firing out between gaps in the boards.

Tonto unfettered a pistol from its rest, afraid to release the boy with more than a single hand. Fire and smoke followed in his wake. Wolves dropped as he cleaved a path toward the people's haven. The men inside ceased their rifle-fire and a cheer rose from the lips of the younger males. The wolf-men backed away from the buildings, wary of the dark man with the deadly, shining bullets.

Ranger

Scout pulled up by the broken porch. Her rider dismounting swiftly as he lugging the youth along behind him. Tonto fired off several shots at a few of the braver beasts who had stepped toward them. A pair of ranchers worked at the wooden slates over the doorframe, wrenching out the iron nails. "Has anyone been injured?" The Indian inquired over his shoulder, keeping a watchful eye on the pacing monsters.

"No' yet," replied a farmer as he took the boy from Tonto's arms. Another man continuing the answer.

"We gots all the women and children in first, then blockaded ourselves in 'ere. We tried to fetch William, but 'is door were latched and he wouldn't answer. I pray he's no been taken already." He pushed the hat back on his head, scratching at his chin in concern.

"Ok," muttered their unlikely ally, popping open his revolver's cylinder to reload. "I'll see if I can't get to him." He slipped a bullet-filled belt over his head and presented it to the man. "Try shooting these."

The rancher pulled one loose, inspecting it. He looked up in surprise, his brow furrowed. "But these is silver."

"That they are, friend," Tonto agreed. "A wise lesson I've learned throughout my years is simply this: sometimes it's best not to ask questions in periods of trial; merely trust." He smiled dryly, slipping onto Scout's back. "Come on, girl."

He nudged her into a trot, and the two hurdled through the increasing circle of werewolves. Some fell as shots rang out through the frenzied afternoon. The rain shower had paused its downpour, but the grey, billowing clouds yet blocked the sun from sight and a hefty wind dashed harshly into ones face.

Tonto leapt from Scout's back, bounding up the wooden steps to the chapel's door. He hastened through the open entrance and ran to the side compartment, finding the entry latched shut as the rancher had stated. He rammed his shoulder into it repeatedly, knocking furiously. "William!?" He bellowed through the door. When no voice replied from within, he slammed a final fist into it and hurried out of the church. There had been a looking-window in the room, correct?

Tonto flew off the porch, skipping most of the steps, and spun a pistol into his hand, halting a wolf that was sneaking up on Scout. He propelled himself around the side of the petite, white-walled building and caught sight of the window. Tonto plastered his face up against the glass, peering inside. He could see Will sprawled out on the floor among his books. The minister looked unconscious, and his chest rose and fell. There was no visible blood or wounding. The Asgaya-wahya either didn't know of his whereabouts or didn't care, for the creatures could have easily broken the weak panes.

Tonto stepped away, judging it best to leave the chaplain there for the time being. He glanced over his shoulder, trying to determine the best place to take up his position. His eyes strayed to the forest off on the horizon, and his heart faltered. Light explosions erupted above the treetops, the timberlands shuddering, and lighting flashed.

Time was running out. The beasts were loose on the town, William was comatose, Kim had most likely been swayed to Vukodalk's side by now, and his silver bullets wouldn't last forever. The settlement would be overrun, Vukodlak would have victory, and if his sister was sent to kill him would he be able to face her down? Would he be able destroy her?

Chapter 20

'Oh, God, I need you,' Kim implored, shielding her face from the spray of darkness Vukodlak spewed at her.

He recoiled as if struck. "Thoughts and prayers are futile!" He flung another burst of power at her, but this time it was weaker.

Kim stepped forward, strengthened. "God, protect me against evil," she mouthed the words.

"Stupid, He can't hear you! You're in my domain now!" Vukodlak grit his teeth and shot a ball of fire at her, but it was a lesser flame than before.

"God, help me to stand." She whispered, advancing further.

"Shut up!" He growled, endeavoring to shove her backward, but she endured the onslaughts without stirring.

"God, use me. Be known," Kim spoke aloud, stepping to the bottom stair of the dilapidated throne. "Reign through the darkness. Show Your light!" She exclaimed fervently.

"No! Not in this place! He cannot be found here!" Vukodlak tried with all his might to remain standing, towering above her, but he was forced to his knees. "You cannot rule this kingdom. It is my realm!" He snarled in a deathly low voice.

"Even the darkest of shadows can be overcome by the Light. Even the deepest stains of sin can be purged."

"Deceit!" Vukodlak attempted to get his feet under him but some authority held him firmly in place as if he were part of the stone.

"Only if you choose not to believe the truth." She lingered at the foot of the throne, but the Spirit proceeded, rising toward the defiant villain.

"Stay back!" He screamed, throwing up his hands and discharging black vapor from them. "I am master in this territory, you hear?! Me!" His eyes flamed with fervor. He began to alter his form, into what Kim did not know for he never got the chance to finish his transformation.

Trapped in-between the body of what she supposed might be a serpent and his humanoid frame, Vukodlak started to fade in front of her eyes; darkness swirling toward him, as if he were drinking it in. She could see his mouth working, but Kim couldn't hear any of the words. The gusts picked up, churning about in an enormous spherical wind formation and whipping her hair in lashing dances above her head. Kim blinked her drying eyes and gasped to breath against the squall. She swiftly dropped to her knees; covering her head, she curled into a tight ball to outlast the storm's angry blasts.

Leaves whisked over her back and tangled in her hair; the hat having long since been lost. She huddled in on herself, hopeful that it was the wise thing to do. Somehow she discerned her part here was over.

Sounds and echoes filtered through the tempest and made their way to her ears. She grimaced, quickly turning her thoughts to Tonto and a prayer was said silently for him to block out the awful noises. Almost too suddenly, all was quiet.

Kim slowly let her hands fall from her head; she cautiously lifted her eyes to survey the woodland clearing. The dark clouds were rolling back, and a little sunlight was drifting into their place. The deep grass swayed with the slight breeze and the throne sat ridged and broken, crumbling where it stood. Vukodlak was nowhere to be seen. A gloomy haze hovered on the top of the stone step where he had last been kneeling, but it too gradually dissipated in the mounting light.

Kim felt faint, clinging to the fragmented steps to help her stand. She brushed the shorter strands of hair from her forehead and set a trembling foot forward. Her eyes squeezed closed as sharp pain streaked up her limb, and an intense pounding resonated in her ears. Kim's left hand reached up to her cheek, and she drew it away warm and sticky with red. She grit her teeth and took another step. Her next glance upward filled her vision with white, but not from the agony. Silver nickered softly, lying down so she could toss a leg over his back and grasp a fistful of his mane.

He straightened, tramping down the trail toward Ranger's Valley; his head held high. Kim clung to his back with her knees, hunching low over his shoulder blades, her head swimming.

Vukodlak had been defeated, yet it was far from over. His followers still accosted the town; if they were not stopped another would rise up to take their leader's place. Every werewolf had to be removed. Even those who were half-wolf.

Tonto stood with pistols flashing, smoke draping his form so that he stood as an imposing silhouette before the saloon doors defending the people. Kim noted, as her stallion cantered down the street, that he would fight until his last shot, but he would not have to. Silver slid to a halt, and she slipped from his back, her adrenaline pumping into her pain-ridden body.

She jogged toward the fray, taking in the situation as she came. Tonto had a perimeter cleared in front of the saloon, but an uncountable quantity of wolf-men still remained. It appeared that they were preparing to launch a mass attack so that he would not be able to keep them all off at once.

Kim slung her hefty belt behind her shoulder, reaching for both revolvers. With a cry she cut into their ranks from behind, dropping a swath of bodies with her shots. One at a time she fired each pistol with lethal accuracy, arousing a shout of triumph from the men and women blockaded inside the saloon. Tonto's heart surged, surely now they could rout the remainder of Vukodlak's forces. Surely victory was with them.

The Asgaya-wahya whose bodies had not withered away into dust were dragged off toward the south. A pit was dug and the corpses had been burned, then the hole was covered over.

Kim perched on the water trough's edge. Her hands splayed on her knees, she watched the men and women bustle about with foodstuffs, good wishes, and offered aid to help with repairs that would begin the following day and extend for weeks after. The phenomena had left grief and misery in its wake but it had also brought the citizens closer together as a unit.

William ambled over, patting Silver as he strolled past and seated himself on the manger's thick lip. He sighed deeply, like one who had finally gotten full after a long meal. "It's over then. He's gone and so are those who sold themselves to his service."

Kim nodded, her throat constricted from the dry air but she managed to speak, "He is." She leaned precariously to one side as her head swooned. She caught her balance before she toppled into the dirt.

"You are the legend child, then." He smiled, gazing out into the bustling crowd. "I did not know if you would be able to complete the task alone."

"I wasn't capable enough on my own. Someone greater than I defeated Vukodlak in the end," she corrected, taking measured breaths.

Will understood what she meant and mentally he raised a silent thanks. "How are you feeling?" He inquired, taking in her full appearance for the first time – the muddied clothing, tangled hair, blood-stained shirt and face, as well as her labored respiration.

"I'll be alright," she reassured, her right hand quickly latching onto the trough's rim, holding herself in place as she wavered on the edge. "Tonto's getting some things to help. Then he'll take me home."

"You don't look okay." He sounded concerned.

"It's but a slight dizziness; it will pass." She assured him, waving a hand in dismissal.

William couldn't believe her, and his misgivings were recognized when Kim slipped forward into the roadway. He caught her before her upper torso collided with the ground. Her eyes were closed and fresh crimson liquid oozed through her open scar. He lifted her gently into his arms, anxiety creasing his brow. She looked very bad indeed, rather pale, and her features were extremely limp.

As Tonto emerged from the mercantile, he spotted the two figures across the dusty road. His hands grew slack, dropping the items he was holding. He rushed from the building, his face flushed and upset. His sister was fading fast.

Chapter 21

Days passed by, and gradually Kim's fever began to ebb. The amount of blood she'd lost had weakened her greatly, but as she rested the strength flowed back. By the fourth passing of the sun she'd woken in a cold sweat, mumbling about some act that needed to be completed. Tonto had gently pushed her back down and his Indian sister succeeded in getting a meager amount of stew into her before she'd fallen into the unconscious sleep once more.

By the close of the week, Kim could stand with some aid, and her vision had ceased to blur. She desired to breath the fresh air, and Tonto had granted her that, permitting her to sit outside of the tipi where she and Silver could spend time together. Will had wanted to pay a visit, but Tonto had refused him, not every human of the white race was allowed in the village of Hungdi.

In her spare time, Kim had retrieved sheets of bark from the trees closest to the village and had taken to writing. She'd requested that Tonto bring her books, and he'd complied, borrowing several from Will for she was eager to learn more of this God who'd saved them all.

A month passed before Kim could make an appearance in the settlement, so that when she did it appeared mostly rebuilt. With the walls back in place, hitching posts stuffed into the soil, new railings on the porches, and much more welcoming people; it seemed an entirely different town.

Ranger

Kim didn't remove her mask even though she doubted it would matter too much anymore. To the people she was the lone Ranger and her disguise was her symbol. Once she took it off she'd undoubtedly disappear into the crowds, and no one would recognize her. They needed the reminder her concealed face brought, a token of what they had come through together. For the time being she would continue to wear it to symbolize hope.

On a cool, crisp morning, when the saplings leaves began to tinge red in the autumn chill, Tonto and Kim took a ride through the forest on their course to Ranger's Valley.

Tracing the timeworn path they had always traveled, Kim breathed deeply of the air and memorized each passing view. Moseying leisurely toward the town, they meandered their way toward the secondary trail which stagecoaches normally used to journey to the city in the north. Kim had wanted to see it again. Now that she had come through her past, there were still a few things that needed to be set at rest before the end.

They stumbled onto the slightly overgrown tracks with ease, Tonto halting Scout and drawing away to wait. Kim continued on ahead.

She rode further into the woodland, taking to the disturbingly familiar track. Though she had only covered it once, Kim knew it well. After a time she called Silver to a halt and dismounted, asking him to remain there. She went on alone.

The timbers thickened all about her and Kim's mind flew back. Eyes, eyes in the forest and dark shadows chasing them. The horse's screams, the driver's cries; here was where the coach had swung about when the horses went wild. She paced the deep ruts that tore into the soil; their wheels had shattered here. She bent and touched a splinter from a spoke that stuck into the ground like a stake.

The creatures had attacked over there, stealing her family and forcing her to leap from the carriage. She had run so hard she thought her lungs would burst. Kim retraced the trail she'd taken with her memory and her feet began to churn with motion. Rapidly she picked up pace and in moments she was sprinting down the path of her memories, the past as her pursuer.

Her breath came hard, and in the near distance Kim could see the clearing she'd taken refuge in. Her legs provided a final spurt of energy, and she flew up to the edge of the dell, halting before she entered the glade. Kim gazed in at the sun-speckled grass that surrounded Tonto's mother's cross. It marked her grave, and it also marked another's.

She tread lightly over the boundary into the opening, her eyes filled with memories, sounds, and smells of that night. She flinched as a creature threw a clawed paw at her mind, her heart beating faster. Kim took a deep breath and knelt down beside the cross. She closed her eyes, the tears of her memories and her past decreasing silently. Her

Ranger

cheek thrummed and grew warm. Sobs noiselessly filled her being as she remembered and forgave.

Light sloped oddly in through the thin slant of the trees when Kim finally stood and hiked her way back to Silver and from there to Tonto. Her brother observed her coming from a distance, mounting back up onto Scout and saying not a word when she rejoined him. He sent her an encouraging smile, though in his heart he was breaking. His spirit felt crushed, but he knew there could be no other way around the inevitable; Kim would not allow it.

The pair cantered into town side by side; one dark-skinned, one darkly clad and masked. The silver bullets, gun belts, and pistols had been left behind; those would be needed no more after today.

William came out to meet them as they trotted passed the church building, the two riders being obliged to break and trade formalities. Kim hadn't wanted to halt in town, just journey through it one last time. She hadn't wanted to say goodbye, so she didn't.

They were soon on the road once more, passing by several work teams who still toiled at repairing the lesser holes in the building's outer walls. The crews stopped their labor to wave, hailing them as heroes, the lone Ranger and her Indian. Kim tipped her hat in recognition and Tonto gestured back in return, but they didn't halt, there was still a long way yet to go.

Evening was falling quickly and the sun dipped well below the horizon. The dark figures rode due south, out past the Asgaya-wahya burning pit and burial grounds. The stars faded into view and the moon shone down on their path – the stallion's coat reflecting the light in a glowing manner. The nocturnal animals rose and went about their nightly routine, somewhat thrown off by the travelers passing.

Kim's heart was heavy; she knew this night was her last and this her final ride. They were journeying to the quarry to end it all; she was the only wolf that remained. Though merely a half-blood, she was still a threat. She couldn't control herself, and she would live forever unless her body was purged of the heinous parasite that existed inside her.

The horse's hooves created a rhythmic sound as they crunched over the gritty dirt and pebbles. Kim's mind lulled into a void, and a partial sleep enveloped her. The dreams that followed were peaceful and her soul was at rest so that when Tonto shook her shoulder to rouse her, she felt relaxed and ready. They dismounted and left Scout behind at the lip of the mine; Silver had been injured by the wolf-men and Kim reasoned that somehow made him half wolf as well. Rashadi hadn't specified much about his wound.

They descended into the quarried depths, the light of the full moon guiding their steps over the precarious, rocky paths. They gained the bottom and marched into the wide open spaces. Kim's eyes slowly took in the walls and caverns all about them. If something happened and Tonto had trouble drawing the poison from her – if she didn't perish right away and instead became a beast – hopefully the pitfalls would contain her until the silver had done its work.

Absolute calm washed over her. She stroked Silver on the muzzle and spun large eyes on Tonto. He looked horrified. Perhaps she should have requested someone else to come from the village and do this, but it was far too late now.

The moonlight flowed and sparkled over thousands of silver shards imbedded in the rock. Kim lingered in the hush and thought of her life; Tonto stood and feared taking it.

Kim paced forward. Tonto followed, hesitating, and watched Kim slip the saddle packs off Silver's bare back. She towed the tattered garments from within and arranged them in a pile. Kim strode away and he knelt by the cluster of fabric to light it. Presently she returned, a long, skinny shard of metal in her hand. She passed it off to Tonto who began heating it over the flames.

Kim observed him, her lips moving soundlessly as she recalled the words of Rahsadi: *"The only method I know that could end her fate as she is, half human half beast, is if she were to turn fully into an Asgaya-wahya, or unless her scar was melted away with silver. I don't believe this would have the desired effect however, for you must apply the hot metal to the wound directly and I fear that would destroy the one who was infected."*

Tonto's face was set in a grim guise, though his hands were trembling even as he held the dagger of silver over the fire. He had to melt away the poison with it, but how? How could he risk her dying?

The metal turned a pasty white and Kim noted Tonto still held it there above the blaze, unblinking. "I suppose we should do what we came to do." She cast a side-long glance at her partner and strode into the glow of the moon, the horse following behind her.

Tonto nodded, removing the barb from the flame. A single tear slipped past his eye.

Above the sky darkened, a few stars streaked across the high heavens as if in mourning and below the silence reigned supreme.

Epilogue

I can remember the pain, but I can't describe it. However, it was not as completely overwhelming as the moments when I felt alone and abandoned by everyone, even God. This time I knew God was with me.

I made certain Tonto melted my wound first. We didn't know what was going to occur, and if Silver had perished I don't think I could have borne it. As it is, we're both very much alive, though we're also very much changed.

Silver no longer walks as he once did and he cannot run any more, but my stallion can still bear my weight on his back.

Even though I was altered physically when the venom entered by body, I have not transformed now that it is removed from within me. I still stand tall as any man, strong as an ox, and my scar yet remains. Though now it has a gleam to it if the light shines just right upon it.

I don't recall what happened after Tonto brought the flaming-white blade to my face and began to cut my flesh. I know I cried out and I then passed from the realm of reality. I also realize I am healed; something inside of me has changed. Where there was numbness that threatened to grow and overcome me once again, it is no more, not even the smallest portion. I have been purged of the curse and am no longer immortal.

I have turned in my mask for my real face and the dark clothes for that of my Indian attire.

Although I still stick out like a broken arm in the settlement, people don't recognize who I am, or who I was. For that I am grateful.

They still speak of the lone Ranger at times. Though now she is more of a passing memory as no one has seen her since that fateful afternoon when she rode off toward the south, never to return. Many argue whether or not my Silver was her horse. Most have come to the conclusion that simply because he looks the part doesn't mean he is. They claim that her stallion could run, swifter than the desert winds. They said he could run and this horse cannot.

They've accepted me for the stranger I am and are willing to see what I have to offer this town. They have also begun to tolerate Indians coming into the shops for trade and the sharing of knowledge, thanks to Tonto, I believe, and his acts of bravery in defending the people from the wolf-men.

I've taken up residence across the street from my old home and have decided to take a different surname. I am no longer a Ranger, I guess I never was. Now I am Kim Rajya. Tonto says in his tongue it means Kingdom, like my father – the kingdom brother.

Tonto comes to town every day to visit. We'll speak of future things, ride, or hunt in the forest together. Though not by blood, we are brother and sister until death do us part. I could not ask for a closer friend and companion.

Ranger

Will has been instructing me on the ways of God and how I am to follow Him blindly and fully. I have changed in countless ways. Yet, I believe I am the only one who comprehends and grasps it to the fullest. I am so different and yet no one distinguishes it except Tonto, William, and myself.

I go to the saloon at times to see old acquaintances and on rare occasions to meet new ones, to have a glass of water, and to listen to stories of the old days, as they are now entitled. I went there just last afternoon and the tale I heard is one worth retelling.

And even if no one else ever hears it, at least I shall know it. Sometimes the stories that truly mean something are the ones that never go beyond closed doors; the ones that never get told. But it shall be on no account of mine that they are not recited, I shall make sure of that.

I walk into the slightly smoky outer room. The sounds of many voices all conversing together greet my ears, and I stroll over to my usual seat on the far left end of the bar. The tender behind the table dips his chin in my direction and shortly after my liquid arrives. I thank him kindly and settle back to watch the various individuals. People and I have never quite gotten along as might be natural, so I choose to stay further away if I don't need to be involved.

A stagecoach arrived today from the west, heading for the city in the north. They had stopped in Ranger's Valley for supplies and to spend the approaching night in our hospitable, dusty town. The teamster of the carriage sits near the bar now, peering into a cup.

I examine him and my eyes narrow. It's as if I know him from somewhere, but I can't place it. The double-hinged doors at the front of the saloon swing wide and young Dirk saunters in with an expression to lift even the saddest of spirits. He beams his winning grin, strolling up to the bar.

"What'll it be?" The man filling glasses inquires, leaning his elbow on the counter.

"Something weakish fer pa; you know how he ain't supposed ta drink. But we got's our herds about up en even ta what they used ta be 'gain." He grins and winks. "He wants ta celebrate a bit."

"And fer yerself?" The bartender pulls a squat, rotund jug out from under the tabletop and thunks it down between them.

"I could eat somethin' hot, if ya got's anythin'." He decides, removing the hat from his head and shoving it into his belt.

"Got some soups left over, still hot as the daylight," the man replies.

"Fine." Dirk smiles, seating himself and restlessly glancing over at the coach driver beside him. "I hear yer headed ta the city. Fine place that. Used ta be dangerous ta get there though, not no more."

The carter straightens up. "That a fact?" He probes, genuinely curious. "How so?"

Ranger

Dirk swings his legs about so he can face the man and starts his explanation with wide eyes. "Once a long time ago, there were beasts that haunted the trails that cut through the woods just up yonder." He hooks his finger in the forest's general direction. "They were's fearsome creatures, black and deadly, foul and angry. They killed our governor and 'is family, God rest their souls, while they were travelin' ta the city. No one ever thought anything was too curious 'bout it, 'til the monsters came an' slaughtered my Papies and mine cows. Skinned 'em all and left their carcasses, didn't even bother ta eat 'em." He spits to the ground in disgust.

"That's a shame," the driver agrees.

"Indeed, but what followed were worse. The beasts came 'n attacked the town, rippin' up the ground and destroyin' porches and walls. They even took a hostage, the minster. T'were dreadful. Then one day, we was fixin' to work on repairing some of the buildings when the monsters came back, a full pack of 'em. We got most ebverybodies in here, and commenced to shootin' at 'em. But they didn't die."

The man's expression appears skeptical at the least. "You must a missed 'em," he offers as explanation.

"Naw." Dirk shakes his head. "I saw one man's bullet go straight into the snarling beasts mouth. Didn't hardly make it weaken. They just kept comin'. We thought we'd all be dead but out of the gloom rides an Indian. Dark and brave he drives through 'em like they was water and he were Moses. Partin' like a curtain a grain afore a sheerer. He shot 'em and they died afore him. Silver, sir, he used silver."

"Silver?" The teamster muses.

"Yessiree. Purer metal there weren't never, and it worked like magic on these creatures, kilt 'em faster than you could shoot 'em almost. Anyway, we was still outnumbered, the Indian's bullets was runnin' low and we though fer sure they'd swamp 'im. But low ta the north comes riddin' from the forest a masked lady, tall as a man and stronger than a thousand of 'em. She rides a horse that's whiter than snow and swifter than the wind. She came ta the rescue, taking them beast down from the rear with her own silver bullets and she goes ta! Hoi, sir I wish you could'a saw'd it! Twas a sight ta remember." Dirk's face beams and he slaps a hand down on the countertop.

"What happened then?" The visiting fellow queries, his brow furrowing.

"Then we got's the town back ta gether, and they left." Dirk answers, his face going slack.

"Just up and vanished?" The coach driver exclaims.

"We saw 'em once more, the Indian and the mask woman." He shakes his head. "And then never again. They disappeared."

"Where to?"

Dirk shrugs; the bartender has returned and he places a bowl of steaming soup before the young

Ranger

man. "I don't rightly know. Nobody does. They say she'll come back when we need 'er. When trouble calls, she'll come ridding in with the sunrise. You'll drive safely through them woods tomorrow because of 'em, because of the lone Ranger."

I stand up; it's time to leave. I step towards the door and hear someone calling after me. I turn, almost afraid they'll recognize me. "On yer way already, Kim?" The bartender asks politely. I nod.

"I believe I should be getting home about now. Thank you for the drink." I walk across the wooden-slated floor and push through the swinging entrance. I'm back outside, blending in with the townspeople the best I can, and they still don't know who I am or who I was. I feel safe.

I walk along the connected porches down the rows of shops and homes, gazing out across the dusty plains. My thoughts swim slowly into the shore of my mind.

So they say I've disappeared. They think I'm lost to this world and its people. They call me the lone Ranger. And they even say I'll come back and save them from the dangers that roam here, more numerous than the sands of time.

They say this is who I am.
Do I believe them?
Yes, I do.

The End

Word/Name Guide and Pronunciations:

- *Hominem lupus* ~ Man-wolf in Latin.
- Oginali ~ (O-gi-na-li) friend.
- Agateno ~ (A-ga-te-no) Scout.
- Vukodlak ~ (Vu-ko-dul-ak) Werewolf.
- Asgaya-wahya ~ (As ga-ya-way-ya) Man-wolf.
- Awinita ~ (A-win-ita) Fawn in Native American.

Slang Words and Sentences:

- Bang-up ~ first rate. "They did a bang-up job."
- Blowhard ~ braggart, bully.
- Bosh ~ Nonsense.
- By hook or crook ~ to do any way possible.
- Chisel, chiseler ~ to cheat or swindle, a cheater.
- Dry gulch ~ to ambush.
- Get a wiggle on ~ hurry up!
- Hobble your lip ~ shut up.
- The whole kit and caboodle ~ the entire thing.

Acknowledgments

Thanks are in order for all the amazing people who encouraged, helped, and otherwise just put up with my craziness all throughout this novel. I'm sure not everyone will make it into this section of the book as I would not have room for all of you. But even if you don't see your name scripted below know that each one of you helped me in too many ways to count.

I've read so many good books and each one inspired me in some way, be it small or large. Thanks to all the authors who didn't give up when the book wouldn't write itself, when the editing seemed so impossible you wondered why you even thought writing was possible, and even when your first book didn't sell the way you hoped. Thank you for your perseverance.

They put up with me on my good days and haven't yet killed me on my bad ones; my family is most amazing to have to deal with me and survive, as well as be encouraging. Mom, Dad, Leah, Daniel, and Andrew, thank you all for your patients and love.

Special thanks to Daniel who said things that really set my mind to rolling. Werewolves and silver bullets for instance. Be wary what you say around me, it just might end up in a book. ;)

All those wonderful sisters who've been there for me to make me laugh and smell sassafras or cry and pray for me, each one is a blessing and one of the greatest gifts from God: Ashley, Tori, Leah, Ophelia, Kya, Bridget, and Meg.

This also goes for all those crazy brothers I have as well; wonderful blessings in my life: Daniel, Andrew, Robert, and Caleb.

There's this place, it's deep underground and filled with lots of crazy, inventive elves. But no matter how far away we each live, how different our lives are, and how strange people think we are to say we have friends who we've never met, we're all united beneath a common banner. The banner has the symbol of a cross and below that the emblem of a writer (and possibly below that a Lord of the Rings icon…Just kidding ;)) But we each share a passion and a desire, we each have separate dreams and hopes for our lives and yet we all manage to encourage and uplift one another – be it through prayer or simply reading and critiquing each other's work. I'm honored to be called one among this great company. Shout out to all the elves of the Underground! You all are simply amazing; God is doing great things in each of you. Endurance and Victory!

Oh my proofies, if only there was a way to express my thanks, but I can't describe it. You all have been an amazing part of this book, maybe even more so then me. Kya, Aunt Theresa, Ophelia, Mom, and my unexpected but greatly appreciated proofies: cousin Julie and Caleb (Who is also my "fight-scene consultant").

Sometimes I can be picky about what I want for my book cover, other times I have no idea. This time was both of those combined but Robert got 'er done! And it's exceedingly epic! Thank you so much, you have fabtaculous patience with me. *hands cupcake* ^_^

And most of all, to whom all the praise, honor, and glory is due, my Lord Jesus Christ. Some days I feel dejected or lost, but each day without fail He gives me joy; a happy bubbling delight of being alive in His world, for His delight, on the road following His plan, for His glory. A hope and a peace that no matter what happens He has a plan for everything I do and everywhere I go. To God be the glory, great things He has done. I've seen them in my own life and in those around me. I pray this book might be a reminder of some of the great things He has done in my life and the hope of what He has yet to do. Amen.

About the Author

Trista Vaporblade is an avid reader, writer, actress, elf, pirate, ranger, and Follower of the Way. She has been writing stories since she was in 1st grade and is the published author of *Quest for the Swords of Healing.* It is said that she can be found in a land far from here, a place not many people discover and even fewer understand; the land of her own imagination. Trista can also be seen roaming the halls of the Underground (www.heedtheprophecies.com), blogging about her world of wonder - (www.tristavaporblade.blogspot.com), or simply dancing in the bright summer sun outside in her backyard. When you pick up a book of Trista's you pick up a book of epic adventures and heroic character in which the good triumphs over evil, but sometimes the cost is far greater than you could ever imagine...

Also from Trista Vaporblade:
(Coming soon)
Ransomed
✳
A Novel

Living like a street rat in the village of Tor, Arlania doesn't think things can get any worse, or better. Her whole life, all she's longed for is acceptance, to have friends, maybe even a family. Though this longing drives her, all it manages to yield is despair; for the people of Tor will have nothing to do with this teenaged girl. This child they've tried again and again to drive off, the girl with the strange gifts – this person they believe is cursed.

One day, however, the tables are turned when a mysterious, cloaked stranger comes to Tor seeking the girl the villagers spurn. Cryptic in his ways and refusing to reveal anything more than the barest of details, he promises Arlania what she's always wanted – if she'll but accept the terms. With little hesitation, she agrees to his odd pact, and the journey that will ultimately lead to her death begins.

As the two travel across rocky mountains, thread their way out of a forest inhabited by creatures as old as time, and dare an attempt to cross the Evenmornt, they find there is more in common between them than they had first thought.

But when all strength has been taxed to the last, trust has been shattered by a thief in the night, and all things Arlania had once held dear are discarded, will she find that the love she always dreamed of is not what she really thought it would be, or what she truly desires? Could it be that this thing she's obsessed over is just a foggy impression of what she needs, and is it this same thing that will inevitably lead her to the gates of doom? (Authors note: This is not a romance)

#113
The Killing Ring

Every year a new group comprised of thirteen members is chosen from among the best; one individual for each of the outlying villages surrounding Tysilio. The Priddyn games are dangerous, but necessary to determine just who is the most qualified for the group. Without these teams and without the prized sap they collect, life on Priddyn Taro would cease to exist.

When a new team is selected in the ninth annual Priddyn games, things begin to change; slowly at first. Dominos start to fall when Verndari, selected to be the protector of the group, stumbles upon a secret government facility. Within, scientists work feverishly to produce a supplement that can be substituted into the populaces food supply in place of the precious sap. Without the sap in the food supply the people's health is at stake, and quickly sickness takes hold of many.

Verndi finds herself in a dangerous position when she tells her teammates about her discovery and somehow it leaks back to the government officials. Sent on just another ordinary collecting mission, Verndi's group finds themselves no longer in the Coed ring – the second ring and the only other "safe" loop on Priddyn – but in the Dilaith ring; or, the Killing ring.

No human being has ever survived this ring; wild beasts run loose, things none of them have trained to defend against; water, plants, the seasons and weather have all changed. Everything they once knew, or thought they did, is different. Can the thirteen mange to make it back to the Bywyd ring alive? And if they do, will they be willing to stand up against the oppression pressed upon the people?

Over cliffs, down mountains, into forests and beyond, that's where adventures take you; but sometimes they can lead you further still…

The Ice Blade Histories

(Frost Laden, Snow Fall, Blizzard)

Legend tells of warriors, old as time, that have passed into lore and are never to return. These men were solid in their values, true to their morals. They held justice in the palms of their hands, mercy in their words, and they fought to uphold these virtues. They carried the Ice Blades, magical swords of great power and strength, but the warriors never used them for ill.

Legend also says that one of their own departed from the ranks. And taking up the lowly mantle of storyteller, he retold the histories of the warriors. These things he could not hold secret in his heart, for he had a great need that drove him to tell the world of the good that still remained, something to hold and cling to. But the accounts were pushed off, turned away; they were merely stories, yarns of great beauty that could never be true.

Things that were once greatly honored were cast off, valor and virtue were shrugged into the deepest pits and left to lie there, truths that ought to have been clung to were lost, and lies that fester and the injustices that were meant to be slain at birth were taken and rooted inside, to deeply too be removed.

A power rose from the darkness known simply as the Guards, men who were deemed to be upright and noble. That is until a young man joined the ranks of the guild and learned for himself the truth behind their secret meetings, their great power, and their elite soldiers. He is staggered to discover that his heroes are murderers and cutthroats, liars of the worst kind. His world is shattered and his only hope is found in an old, dying man who imparts to the lost youth the secret of the Ice Blade Warriors.

Taking to the hidden road with his sister, Elorum, and Tal, his childhood friend, the young man sets off to find justice and real truth. He passes through a reality devastated by the lies of the enemy, lured into the death hold of evil, but his journey is no longer just to find the forgotten warriors, now it is also to find himself.

The world is shifting, pain and destruction run as a dear friend waiting to stab you in the back, and nothing will ever be the same again. Unless the threesome can find these warriors of old, unless they can reveal the message of hope to the people, unless they can repress the evil that is deepening and growing, unless...

What lurks in the shadows beyond their doorstep? Times have changed far more than they ever could have imagined, life is no longer revered, love is no longer sacred, and out there death awaits its next victim. They are being hunted and that which stalks them will never cease until the three trying to save this broken world have sealed its doom...

The Guardian Elf Scrolls, Book 2, The Nameless

The Guardian's return to the realm of their forefathers, Ømälœ, is ill-timed and the hearts of many are sick with grief. As they flock into their longed-after homeland, Vorn's forces assail them on all sides but help ensues from places unlooked to. Routed, the hybrids flee from their foes, but not without spoils from the battle to present to their black-hearted master.

In need of supplies for their journey to the capital, the Guardians masquerade as their enemies and sneak into a nearby village. But things don't always go as planned. Trials push and pull at the tight weave of the eight's bond to one another and doubts mount within. Disputes and disagreements as to their plan of action drives a wedge amid their group, splitting them in their choices.

Doubts rise in the young mind of a hybrid who serves under Vorn and his thoughts constantly stray to what would happen if he went renegade. Fears and duties keep his schemes from pulling through and he dreads the day when the master would finally learn of his treachery.

Phantoms lurk in the dark shadows of the woodlands, hybrid patrols and soldiers keep watch with deadly purpose, and Vorn is not unprepared for the inevitable coming of his bitter rivals.

Even if the eight can get into the shape-shifter's layer, even if they manage to make it past his many lines of defense, they shall have to face something new before they can re-claim the prize Vorn's minion's stole; one known as The Nameless.

Adventures can be your greatest companion or your worst enemy; either way they stretch you, test your metal, and in the end you wind up changed. And perhaps not always for the better…

Now Available:

The Guardian Elf Scrolls, Book 1,
Quest for the Swords of Healing

A storm that heralds the coming of an army of creatures that strike fear and death into those that behold them. A Dark lord who orders a force of thousands in search of his quarry that has escaped him for ages. That is until he found a scroll that revealed the

Ranger

location of his foes, Earth would soon feel his looming presence.

Actors for years, eight teenagers work alongside hundreds of others in an attempt to create a medieval film of astounding battle sequences, that is until something puts them off their schedule. Until someone blows up their studio, until two opposing forces divide the teens in half, until mind-blowing possibilities are presented to them of who they really are, and until their world is shaped into another.

Sent on a quest to find relics of years gone by, the young warriors encounter things that send them reeling, surpass the bounds of reality, and remove all doubt of their past.

Without knowledge of what the relics really look like, or where they lie hidden, the teens embark on the journey of a life time to help save their world, or send it into ultimate catastrophe.

What will happen to the teenagers in this time where combat is deadly real, and if they make a wish death waits to claim them?

Adventures are not always what you make them out to be, sometimes they are so much more...

Trista Vaporblade

Made in the USA
Lexington, KY
15 September 2014